SURROUNDED

BY

Secrets

USA TODAY BESTSELLING AUTHOR
MANDY HARBIN

For more information, please join Mandy Harbin's Newsletter!

To the readers who stayed with this series over the years. Jack is for you. I don't mean that as an insult. I think you will finally fall in love with him after this.

CHAPTER ONE

JACK STARED at the photo he'd taken from his father's desk weeks ago, when he'd stumbled upon it during a conference call with Lillian Caldwell. He'd been verbally sparring with the infuriating—and mesmerizing—neighbor about her desire to work for his family's tree business full-time, rather than contracted as needed, when he'd discovered this picture of Lina Woods.

Mom.

She was frozen in time with several other people he hadn't recognized. She looked beautiful, though. Timeless. Of course, he'd always known she was a captivating woman. Up until her death, Lina's presence in any room commanded attention. And his father, Thomas, was always putty in her paws. They were mated, and a mated pair's bond was an unbreakable force fueled by love and respect, a lesson that had only been reinforced by watching Jack's brothers mate with their females.

His parents had never discussed the dynamics of their mating because it was a personal experience meant to be shared with no one. Besides, talking about mating and their heritage was pointless because Thomas's parents had died when he was young, the history of their kind dying with them. It seemed Jack and his brothers would be doomed to struggle with the possibility of mating on their own. But Josh, Toby, and Rob had beaten the odds. They'd all found mates who loved them. Eric's story was another matter entirely. He'd taken a mate against her will, and they'd fought to the death.

Jack figured if he were ever to be lucky enough to find a woman who wanted to spend her life with him, it would go one of two ways.

Thankfully, the compound Ariel had created seemed to be working. *Now.* Krista had coerced her sister into coming onto the land, and once she fussed around with the mood recipe to where Jack could stomach it, he'd been doing well on it—though he'd never truly forgive himself for stopping the meds and almost raping his brother's mate. He had a lot to prove to his family after that major fuckup.

And to himself.

Sighing, he put the photo away in his nightstand and grabbed his worn work boots. He needed to talk to Josh about that photo, but the timing just never seemed right. Jack knew the real reason he'd avoided the conversation before was he'd been keeping his nose down, focusing on his work, hoping it might make it easier to face his family. Though hiding behind that mistake was just an excuse. Failure wasn't something he was accustomed to, but he needed to be a man and not a chickenshit. He wasn't known as the hard-ass around here for nothing. Besides, trying to constantly make amends had opened up a whole other can of worms.

Because Lillian Caldwell was getting her wish.

Today was her first day as an official employee of his family. And hell if that didn't make his life even that much more problematic. She was fucking beautiful, a true vision of all that he'd ever thought made up the physical appearance of his ideal woman, curvy and blonde. Damn, he was in some serious trouble now. All those conference calls with her had done nothing but worn out his right hand for hours. He'd thought that after attacking Ariel he'd be a cold fish, but oh no, he couldn't be *that* lucky. His dick still knew what it wanted, and his lion still yearned for a mate. But his brain knew better, and this had catastrophe written all over it. Not only did he get to see his personal siren in the flesh, but he got to work with her. Rather, she got to work for him. Indefinitely. God, the last thing he needed to add to his mistakes was a sexual harassment lawsuit.

Lillian Caldwell, in all her physical perfection, was off-limits. His dick, and his lion, would just have to get over it.

———

LILLIAN LOOKED IN THE MIRROR. Red thong? Check. Matching red bra? Check. She cupped her breasts and shook her head. Lordy, her boobs were too big.

It'd be nice if she could walk into Victoria's Secret and buy off the shelf, but unfortunately, she had to get her bras at the big-girl store. At least she'd found a sexy one. Knockers this size usually required her to wear a grandma bra. But that was unacceptable for today. She needed something sexy in case the hottie with the body got her clothes off. Jesus H. Christ, but Jack Woods was sex on a stick.

And come hell or high water, she'd have him in her bed. It wasn't often she set her sights on a man, but there was just something about Jack that got her body humming. It'd been too long since she'd been truly pleased by a man, and she was long past due for a righteous big O.

There was only one real reason Lillian had strong-armed the Woods clan into giving her a permanent position with their tree farming business, and she wasn't too much of a flake to admit that. She wanted to see the hottie with the body nekkid.

She hadn't lied when she told them there weren't that many jobs around here, but they were right in that she didn't need the money. They had offered her dad plenty of money for his land. She'd tried to stop the sale at first, but her dad really did need a break. He seemed so distracted lately, so she hoped unloading the responsibility of their tree farm would help him. It definitely freed up his time.

He had flown out yesterday to visit her grandma for a couple of weeks. Thankfully, when she'd told him she'd taken a full-time position with the Woods family, he hadn't seemed that upset. Actually, he was almost happy for her. Little did he know that selling their land had opened up another, more physical, opportunity for her, too.

An opportunity she was going to grab by the balls.

Not that she didn't have other offers. Lillian had broken up with her ex-boyfriend a few months ago, but the dickhead was still hounding her about going out again. Maybe she would if David knew how to please her sexually, but he was a little too passive in between the sheets. The notches on her belt were limited to just a few men since she was incredibly choosy, but David had been a major disappointment. He was tall with dark blond hair and green eyes. Muscular. Tanned. Gorgeous. But when it came to sex, he was a little too submissive for her liking. *Ugh*, and when he came, the sounds he made were a total turnoff: whiny, whimpering, weak. Such a contradiction to his strong, manly presence out of bed. Jack wouldn't sound like that. She just knew it. He'd growled at her several times during their arguments, and each time her panties got wet. He just oozed sexual dominance.

And that was just what she needed.

She slipped on her tight jeans, put on a lacy shell, and then donned a fitted flannel shirt, leaving the top few buttons undone so the camisole, and her cleavage, peeked through. She shifted. Thongs weren't really work attire, but she'd deal with the discomfort. She was on a mission.

No pain, no sex.

She slipped into her boots. She'd considered trading them out for something a little more fashionable, but she was going to be there to work. Wearing new shoes was a rookie mistake, so if she wanted to be taken seriously, she'd have to wear her old work boots. Besides, blisters were not sexy, and new shoes had to be broken in before being acceptable as work-wear attire.

Lillian grabbed the keys to her four-wheeler and trotted out. She didn't need to bring a purse or anything else since she'd faxed her driver's license and Social Security card to them last week. And since she lived next door, she wouldn't have to pack a lunch.

She climbed onto the wheeler and started it. After revving it a few times, she kicked it into gear and headed down the trail to the Woods estate. Within a few minutes, she'd passed the gate that had been left open and made it through the clearing. Surprisingly, she wasn't feeling nervous at all.

Under normal circumstances, she didn't chase men, but for some reason, she knew she'd have to make the first move if anything were to happen with Jack. And that helped her resolve.

There he was. Standing next to a large pine tree that started a section of new growth stood the hottie with the body. She pulled right up to him and killed the engine. Okay, so there were some butterflies swimming in her now because, holy Christ, he was way hotter in person.

"Lillian." He nodded to her and took her hand as she started off the wheeler.

His voice was like rough silk. She loved hearing him talk over Skype, but that paled in comparison to hearing him speak now. And the feel of his hand sent electrical sparks arcing through her. Oh yeah, she was going to fuck him. Tonight.

"Hello, Jack."

Once she was clear of her four-wheeler, he let go of her hand and stepped back while he slid that hand through his hair. His gorgeous blue eyes held her.

He cleared his throat and shifted. "I apologize for being so difficult about you working here. I shouldn't have—"

She waved her hand, dismissing the comment. "No need. I'm here." She took a step closer. "Now where do you want me, Jack?"

She smiled at him and raised a brow, knowing her comment was borderline suggestive, and hoping like hell he thought so, too.

He looked to the right and indicated the nearest patch of trees. "I figured I'll show you around the farm and tell you the years when each section is to be harvested and replanted, make sure you know your way around before setting you loose."

Hmm, he didn't even flinch at her suggestive tone. And she had her hands on her hips, thrusting her bodacious tatas in his direction. She wasn't used to playing the vixen. Maybe she was doing it all wrong. A panicked thought of her making a fool of herself in front of her new boss almost paralyzed her. Then she chastised herself. She wouldn't know if she didn't try. But she needed to take it down a notch. This was just going to be harder than she'd thought.

Lillian nodded and tried to seem nonchalant. "Sounds good. I'll just follow you on my wheeler."

When she turned to her four-wheeler, she noticed a tic in his jaw. Odd.

"You shouldn't wear perfume to work. It can attract insects," he practically barked at her.

At that, she had to laugh as she straddled her ride and looked over at him. "Don't worry, big guy. I know the drill. I don't wear perfume. There's nothing artificial about me."

Heat flared in his eyes before he quickly banked it. Well, well, well, maybe this wasn't going to be so hard after all. Time to sink or swim.

"Since this is my first job outside of my family business, I think drinks are in order tonight. You can pick me up at eight."

She started her wheeler, not letting him answer. She saw the warring in his eyes. He was going to try to turn her down.

Good luck with that, hottie with the body. Tonight, you are mine.

CHAPTER TWO

Jack stomped to the dining room of the main house. Drinks with Lillian? Why hadn't he turned her down?

You tried, asshole. She was too stubborn to take no for an answer.

He'd never met a more infuriating woman. Working with her proved just as heated as their conference calls. She'd argued with him on just about everything. From the way they'd spaced out their rows of trees to the types of pesticides they used. She was too fucking opinionated.

And that didn't do a damn thing to cool his ardor. Every time she'd bent over, he'd studied her ass as though he'd be tested on it later. Visions of him ripping off her clothes and thrusting into her bombarded him all day. And her breasts... the online meetings they'd had hadn't done those assets justice. If he wasn't picturing her bent over a log, the wheeler, a rock, or the nearest object so he could take her from behind, he was envisioning her flat on her back, with him shoving his cock between her milky mounds.

He was in serious trouble. His dick had been hard all day, and the knowledge that he'd see her tonight only made matters worse. He'd jacked off in the shower. Twice. The first time he'd come so fast he'd gotten dizzy. The second time took much longer, and the reward was one of the best hand-job orgasms he'd ever delivered himself. Not that his cock was sated.

He pushed open the door, and the muffled chatter and laughter among his family died. Fuck, he hated the weary looks on his sisters-in-law's faces, and the mixed stares he got from his brothers and father. If he was going to get through this night with any dignity, he'd need a drink. Now.

"Hi, everybody," he mumbled as he made his way to the sideboard where the scotch was housed.

"Good evening, son. How did it go today with the Caldwell lady?"

Jack poured his drink and sipped before answering, "Interesting."

"How so?" Josh asked.

Jack turned to face the judges, jury, and executioners. "She complained about everything. Apparently we don't know shit about the business we're in. Go figure." He glared at Josh as he took another drink.

"You'd already assumed it'd be a difficult situation. How did you handle your urge to mate? She's unmated." Ariel stepped toward him as she asked, and he lost a bit of his stubbornness. He wondered if it'd always be like that between the two of them, he the monster to her generosity.

"Not bad. I had, er, moments of difficulties focusing on the job." He shrugged and looked away, not able to make eye contact. "She's a beautiful woman," he murmured.

"She's a bitch," Toby snapped.

"Toby!" Krista screeched.

"What? She is. She wormed her way into our business like she has a reason to be here. If Dad wasn't worried about her screaming discrimination to the authorities, he wouldn't have agreed to this."

Jack's gaze snapped to Toby. He couldn't identify the strange urge that bubbled up inside him at Toby's insult. He just knew it didn't sit right with him. At. Fucking. All.

"Now, Toby. That's not true. We do need help around here, and she's fully capable. You better treat her with respect, son. I won't have it any other way."

Toby growled and turned to his mate. Krista stroked his cheek and whispered to him. Jack watched him put his forehead against hers and nod. Although Toby's words were for his mate, everyone in the room heard his apology.

As Ariel took another step toward Jack, Rob stepped up to her. He didn't blame his brother for being overprotective.

"You're attracted to her," Ariel mused.

He sighed. "I just said she was beautiful."

Mikaela walked over, rubbing her baby bump. "Oh my God, you are. You're usually all, 'I'm claiming the woman. It's my turn. Me Tarzan. She Jane.' But now you're actually a little nervous." She giggled. "This is priceless."

Even through his irritation, he couldn't help but crack a smile at his pregnant in-law. "I am not like that."

"Oh, yes you are. You pound your chest and everything. I'm surprised you don't swing from the branches."

"I may climb a tree or two, but I do not swing on anything," Jack said as he took another swig of his scotch.

"If you're attracted to her, maybe one of us should shadow her instead of you," Josh said. He wrapped his arms around his pregnant wife, feeling his baby, and dropped his chin onto her shoulder as he looked at Jack.

Over his dead body would he allow any of his brothers to take his place. Lillian was his, damn it. Well, not *his* his, but his responsibility, he immediately corrected.

"Look, I'm taking my medicine like a good little boy. I managed to make it through the day without forcing her to do anything the stubborn little vixen didn't want to, and I'm sure I'll make it just fine tonight, too."

"Tonight?"

Jack wasn't sure who all had asked, but it seemed that one word had echoed throughout the dining room. Shit.

"Um, yeah, we're going for drinks tonight. She wanted to celebrate her first real job outside of her family business."

"And you're going?" Rob asked. Why was he smiling?

Jack growled as he stomped over to the bottle of scotch and refreshed his drink. "She didn't give me much of a choice." He took a drink and faced his family. "I tried to bow out, but she wouldn't have it." Another swig. "Kept coming up with reasons why I should that trumped the lame ones I was dishing out." Another. He pitched his voice higher and mimicked Lillian when he said, "'Don't be a douche.' 'I'm not being a douche. I just think it's a bad idea to see coworkers out-side of work.' 'You're just trying to get me to quit. It won't work, big guy. Quit being a chickenshit.'" He stared at his family in awe. "Me, a chickenshit?" Yeah, he was, and had been one around his family of late, but he hated Lillian thinking of him like that.

Everyone in the room was staring at

him as if he'd grown a third eye and sprouted wings.

"What?" Jack snapped.

"Ha, you're in some serious shit, my brotha," Rob said, chuckling.

Jack groaned as he downed the rest of his scotch.

"Looks like you're getting a head start on drinking. Keep that up, and you won't be able to drive," Toby said.

He laughed without humor. "Oh, she thought of that, too. She's having a cab pick us up."

Ariel reached out to touch his arm, and his anger deflated. "I think this is good for you, Jack. You need to interact with women. You are free to leave this land and not have to worry about taking an unwilling mate."

Only because of Ariel was that true. Up until she'd arrived, the unmated Woods men could not be around an unmated woman. If that were to happen, he'd take her against her will. They were mountain lion shifters with a deadly urge to mate. But as long as Jack stayed medicated, it wouldn't be a problem.

And he knew he was out of excuses.

"It's more than that," he said as he placed his empty glass on the table.

"I know." Ariel nodded. "You don't have to say it. But believe me when I tell you, it's not us you have to convince."

She knew he was terrified, and she was telling him that he needed to trust in himself. He didn't know if he could do that. But if only for her, if only for the pain he almost caused her, he'd try.

Jack nodded at Ariel, somber in his resolve.

"Dude, you could so get lucky!" Rob said, breaking the newly found tension.

"Mmm-hmm. Just think, man, you could get some without making a commitment. No-strings-attached fun." Josh wagged his brows.

"Hey! Are you saying you wanted something like that?" Mikaela asked as she twisted in Josh's arms.

Oh shit, her emotions had been on a roller coaster. Jack almost felt sorry for Josh having to endure his pregnant wife's mood swings. But then the anger in her eyes was betrayed by the quiver of her lip.

"Oh, kitten." Josh crushed her to him. "You are my everything. Never doubt that," he mumbled as he kissed the top of her head.

"I think you should have fun," Krista said, taking the focus off Mikaela. "But you better make sure you read her right. If she's not giving you any signals, you better keep it zipped. The last thing I want to deal with is a sexual harassment suit."

At that, Mikaela gasped and pulled away from Josh to face Jack. "She's right, Jack. You better be careful. She's an employee now."

Hell, he knew that. But for all his toughness, he hated seeing a woman cry. Mikaela's lashes were soaked, so he had no desire to defend himself. He just nodded at her.

"Gawd, I hate being pregnant! It's been like a thousand months already." Mikaela wiped at the wetness on her face. "Where's Jeffery with the food? I'm starving."

Josh chuckled. "It hasn't been quite that long, kitten."

"I'll go see what's taking so long," Thomas said at the same time. He turned toward the kitchen.

Smart man. Feed the pregnant woman.

With the first dish that came out,

people started toward the table. Mikaela bolted. Since Josh was momentarily free, Jack grabbed his arm. He'd put off this conversation long enough. He needed Josh's thoughts on the photo of their mother. He couldn't discuss it here, but he could at least get the ball rolling.

"Hold up a sec."

Josh turned to face him. "Yeah?"

"Um, there's something I've been meaning to talk to you about. Can we meet up in the morning?"

Josh frowned. "Does this have anything to do with Lillian? Are you really worried about—"

"No, no. Nothing like that. I just need to run some things by you. In private."

Josh chuckled. "You mean ditch my wife?"

Jack smiled. "No, man. Just in private. Feed her a lot for breakfast, and we can chat while she's napping."

Josh groaned theatrically. "But her morning nap is my *me* time. It's when I get to find my balls and reattach them." They both laughed. "Yeah, okay. I'll talk to you tomorrow, bro."

He and Josh took their seats. Mikaela

was stuffing her face, and everybody was chatting. But Jack couldn't stomach the idea of eating right now. He filled his glass with the scotch on the table. He wasn't normally a lush. But tonight he needed all the courage he could get.

Artificial or not.

———

LILLIAN TUGGED on her dress as she poured another glass of wine. The hottie with the body hadn't gotten to see her sexy red panties and bra, but she'd traded them out for her black set after her shower. Maybe he'd see the red ones tomorrow. She'd also ditched the jeans in favor of something more provocative. If this dress were cut any lower, she'd get a ticket for indecent exposure.

She stumbled a little when she turned too quickly. She was only on her second glass of wine. Or was it her third? She couldn't remember. But she hadn't eaten much today either and had worked her ass off outside all day. If Jack was hungry, she could heat up the chili she'd made the other night, and they both could eat.

Because she had no intentions of them leaving her house.

Nope, that was just an excuse to get Jack over here. She figured he'd be more comfortable with the thought of going out in public, rather than staying in, where it was private. But public wasn't conducive with getting her groove on.

She heard a knock at her door, and she smiled. *Showtime.*

Lillian walked to the door and opened it gently. But the air still locked in her lungs. Damn, Jack was hot! Tight jeans, loosely fitted shirt. Blue. Matched his sexy eyes.

His gaze went right to her breast, and she didn't miss when his tongue peeked out to wet his lips.

Then his gaze shot to hers, and he cleared his throat.

"Good evening." He nodded at her as if this was a formal meeting among colleagues. Poor thing. He was in for a rude awakening.

"Come on in." She turned and left him at the door. "I haven't had a chance to eat. I was just going to heat up some chili."

The door shut behind her, so she figured he'd stepped in.

"We can grab something to eat while we're out."

"No need. This will only take a second."

She heard a low oath from his direction and smiled to herself as she pulled out the bowl of chili from the fridge and dumped it into a pot on the stove.

"I have whiskey, beer, and wine. Make yourself a drink," she called out as she started stirring.

"No, thank you."

She almost jumped at how close he was. She hadn't heard him come into the kitchen.

Lillian turned toward the side as she continued stirring. "How about a game to kick off the evening? Grab the whiskey and a couple of shot glasses out of that cabinet over there." She pointed to her left.

"I thought we were leaving," Jack mumbled as he walked over to where she'd directed him, but it wasn't really a question, so she wasn't going to comment. Before long, he'd figure it out on his own.

She turned the heat to low and walked

to the table where he'd taken his seat. "We each take turns saying something truthful about ourselves. If the other disagrees with that statement, he or she takes a shot."

He frowned at her, but after a few seconds, he nodded. Jeez, good thing she was making all the moves here. Otherwise, she'd never get to see this man naked. It was like asking a stone statue to scoot over. She hoped all her efforts would be worth it in the end. *You better be good in the sack, big guy.*

"I'll start." She picked up the bottle, poured two shots, and pushed one toward him. "I have a period."

Jack huffed. "You know damn well I don't have a menstrual cycle. That's cheating." He picked up his shot glass and tossed it back.

Lillian refilled his glass and tsked. "I never said the truth could easily be applied to both parties."

"All right then. I was born a man."

Lillian chuckled as she picked up her shot glass. "Good one." The liquid burned on the way down, but she managed not to wince. "I'm wearing a dress."

"Fuck," he groaned and picked up his

glass to shoot his liquor. "I'm wearing boots."

She rolled her eyes and took her shot before spouting off another truth she knew didn't apply to him.

Lillian wasn't sure how long this little game continued, the chili long ago turned off. And now, she had to shut one eye to pour the next round of shots to keep from spilling alcohol all over her table. If they kept this up, they'd both pass out before she'd reaped the benefits of this little get-together.

"I'm not horny," she confessed as she stared into Jack's bloodshot eyes.

He stared back, the heat in his eyes from earlier today roaring to life. Lillian felt her heartbeat quicken as she waited for his response. And after what felt like an eternity, Jack let go of his shot glass and moved his hand away, showing her with his actions that he was horny, too.

"My dick has been hard for you all day."

She took a drink because she didn't have a penis and clumsily filled her glass.

"My panties are soaked through, and my nipples ache for you to suck them."

"Jesus," he breathed, taking the shot quickly before standing.

Lillian's legs were having problems working, but she managed to stand before he made his way to her.

She had no other warning.

Jack's mouth slammed down on hers in a fierce kiss that stole her breath. He was biting at her lips when she felt her back hit the wall. Everything was moving in foggy slow motion, but no matter how drunk she was, she knew she'd never been this turned on in her life.

"Fuck, I want you," he groaned into her mouth as he thrust his jeans-clad cock against her panties.

"Then take me, big boy," she breathed.

Jack shoved her dress up around her waist with one hand and yanked the top of her dress down with the other. She felt only air on her naked breast briefly before his mouth descended.

She moaned and held his head to her as he feasted and rubbed herself like a cat in heat against his erection. His rather large erection.

She heard him growl and then felt his

hand wiggle beneath her dress. "Oh yes." God, she needed him to touch her.

But he didn't.

He ripped her panties, and she gasped. Then she heard a zipper, and her pussy flooded.

He sucked her nipple harder before letting go with a wet *pop*, and then kissed his way up her neck to her ear. "Can't wait. Need you. Now."

The head of his dick rubbed her slit, and she moaned when it bumped her clit. He hissed.

"So fucking wet, Lilly."

No one ever called her that. She'd always hated that name, but right now he could call her a toad-frog and she wouldn't care.

He found her opening and pushed. One thrust and he was halfway in. And fucking huge! She moaned. It was so good she didn't know if she could stand it.

"Take it, Lilly. Take all of me, baby." He thrust again, and she gasped. She would've screamed in ecstasy, but he swallowed it with his kisses. He fucked her hard, and she felt her orgasm building faster than it ever had, even for her vibrator.

"Shit! I can't. Not yet." He pulled out, and she whimpered. "Bedroom?"

She pointed out of the kitchen, but he didn't let her speak. His mouth landed back on hers, and he carried her out of the kitchen.

They made it to the bedroom, but not the bed. As soon as Jack cleared the doorway, her back met the rug in front of her bed.

"Gotta taste you."

He pushed her legs open, grabbed her ass, and lifted her as his head lowered. "Oh my God, Jack, Jack," she chanted as Jack licked her as though she was his favorite ice-cream cone and he'd never eat another one again. Then he pursed his lips around her clit and sucked while he pushed two fingers inside her and crooked them, rubbing that sweet spot inside.

She saw stars. Her throat was so hoarse that it took her several seconds to realize it was because she'd been screaming out her orgasm.

And he didn't give her a chance to recover. He picked her up and dropped her onto the bed in one minute. In the next, he'd gotten them both undressed.

"I plan on fucking you all night," he said as he crawled toward her, his cock leaking along her leg, and he settled atop her. He grabbed both her knees and pushed them up to her chest. He looked down at her shaved pussy. "You're going to give it all to me, aren't you, Lilly?"

God, he sounded so sexy when he talked to her this way. This was what she'd wanted, a man who took charge in the bedroom. "All for you, Jack."

He groaned and took her with one hard thrust.

"Harder," she moaned.

"You little vixen. I'll give you what you want when I want to." He left her knees anchored around his arms as he leaned over her and pounded into her hard and fast.

She screamed, loving the feel of him taking her, owning her.

"That's right, baby." He licked her ear as he whispered into it. "Tell me how it feels."

"So. Good," she said with the next two thrusts.

Jack kissed her so hard that she knew

her lips would bruise. And she didn't care. He was groaning so loudly that he felt as though he was growling while he fucked her. His dick was getting harder, and she felt another orgasm building inside her.

"Fuck, I want to bite you." He almost sounded desperate.

Her pussy flooded. He could bite her, pull her hair, do whatever the hell he wanted as long as he didn't stop. Not yet. God, not yet.

"Yes. Do it."

Her pussy flexed, and she knew she was about to go over again.

"Lilly. Oh fuck, oh fuck."

His thrusts faltered.

"Jack, don't stop. So good. So good."

She turned her head to the side, giving him better access to her neck as he kissed it. Lillian was so close she was delirious. She was grinding herself against him, so each time he fucked into her, he got that much deeper.

"Want it. Want you. Fuck, don't wanna stop," he mumbled as he sucked her neck.

"Take it. Take me. Yes, oh yes, you're gonna make me come!"

He roared against her neck and

pounded into her two more times. She screamed as her orgasm hit and felt the first jerk of his cock as he bit into her neck.

She was flying. Never had an orgasm been this intense. All her senses felt heightened while her body drifted to another plane, a mixture of ecstasy and peace enveloping her. When she'd come down, she felt Jack shivering above her, still kissing and licking her now-stinging neck.

She thought she heard Jack say *mine*, but she didn't feel any vibrations against her neck as though he'd spoken. Her drunken mind must've been playing tricks on her. The rasp of his tongue against her neck and the faint metallic smell of blood in the air were the only things she now registered.

She wanted to go another round, but that'd have to wait for another day. Her eyes were too heavy to fight sleep anymore.

CHAPTER THREE

WHO WAS TRYING to pry open Lillian's skull with a pickax? She groaned as she tried to move her hand up to her head to feel if the offender had been as successful in unearthing her brain as it had felt to her. But her arm was too heavy to lift. She'd just have to lie there and suffer the blows.

She tried opening her mouth and breathing through the cotton that had apparently grown on her tongue. *Ugh, whiskey.* What the hell was she thinking getting that drunk last night? She'd be paying for it all day today. She knew better.

Alcohol was evil.

Evil.

God, she needed to pee. She tried shifting in her bed to see if her legs would work or if she'd have to actually crawl to the bathroom, but as soon as Lillian moved, she froze, eyes popping open. *Ouch.*

She immediately shut her eyes to block out the offending sun. Too bright. But the body against her side had her reeling, trying to remember the events of last night.

The yucky taste in her mouth and the pounding in her head confirmed that alcohol was involved. It didn't take a rocket scientist to figure that out. The wall of hard muscle and distinct ache between her legs signaled she'd gotten lucky. Had she gotten desperate and called David? She shifted again.

Nope. David wasn't that tall. This man felt massive. And his frame wasn't the only thing that felt huge, unless that was a Louisville Slugger poking her in the buttocks. No wonder her goodies felt lovingly used. This man was packing a weapon between his legs!

A deep, rumbling groan that could only be one of commiserated existence came from her secret lover. He snuggled closer, his breath fanning her ear.

"Time?"

Holy shit! She knew that voice. Images

of her first day at work and her plan to get Jack Woods in her bed flooded her. Apparently she'd succeeded.

Too bad those memories hadn't come back yet. She'd like to reminisce about what the hottie with the body had done to her last night.

She chanced the wicked sun's rays and lifted a lid to glance at the clock. "It's about half-past nine."

"Ugh. I'm fucking late."

Crap! Her job. "Um, me, too."

He snuggled closer. "I drank way too much. Hell, I don't even remember how we ended up here."

At least she wasn't the only one. "What's the last thing you do remember?"

"Just flashes. I remember playing that drinking game, and then kissing you, and then... oh shit! We didn't use a condom. Fuck, fuck, fuck."

"I can't be sure we did it three times, but I'm sure we did it at least once."

He snorted behind her and nuzzled her neck.

It felt so good she moaned. Or so she thought. Some weird noise came out instead, and she cut it off.

"What the...?"

She felt Jack catapult out of her bed, and she turned to look at him. He looked mortified.

"Holy fucking shit!" he roared as he backed away from her.

What the hell was wrong with him, and why did her throat feel funny after that gurgling noise she'd just made?

"It wasn't a gurgle." Jack was white as a ghost.

"What was it then? And how did you know what I was thinking? I didn't say that out loud."

Jack paced, and she twisted her neck to follow. "Ow." That hurt! She slapped her hand on her neck where it was sore.

"I think you gave me a massive hickey, or I fell into a doorknob sometime last night." Both options were entirely possible at this point.

"Oh, no, no, no, no, no," Jack chanted as walked around like a caged animal. A naked caged animal. Was he just now realizing he'd slept with an employee of his family business? That was an obstacle she'd considered she would have to overcome with him, but apparently something worked last night.

But it seemed as if he were regretting getting to know her on this level, when first thing this morning, he seemed okay with it. Prick.

"Look, big guy. It was just sex."

"You have no fucking idea, Lilly."

"My name is Lilli*an*. Not Lilly."

He stopped and looked straight at her. "You have bigger things to worry about than what I call you, Lillian."

She gasped. "How did you do that?"

He threw his head back and roared so loudly that the hair on the back of her neck prickled. It didn't seem possible for a man to sound so animalistic. She edged toward her headboard and pulled the covers closer to her in a pitiful attempt at protection.

"Just great! First, I attack Ariel, and then I claim you. What the hell is wrong with me? My fucking family is going to disown me. And by God, they should!" He was still pacing, and Lillian didn't think he was actually talking to her but rather venting some nonsense.

"Who's Ariel?"

He stopped and stared at her as if he

wasn't aware he'd said anything. "You'll find out soon enough. Fuck!" He fisted his hands and screamed toward the ceiling.

"Um, okay. Then what's this business about your family disowning you? Because you slept with me?" She put her hands on her hips and glared at him. "This isn't some *Romeo and Juliet* crap. Our families aren't feuding, *Jackson*."

Jack rubbed his hands on his face and pushed them through his hair to grab fistfuls of it. He shook his head while his eyes held her.

"I did something last night. I don't know how we are still alive." He chuckled sadistically. She didn't find his attitude very funny.

"Well, if you remember what happened, then spill it."

"*I bit you.*"

She frowned at him and started to open her mouth, but he shook his head.

"*I wanted to bite you. I asked, and you said I could.*"

"How—" She cut herself off. This was nuts! If she could think clearly, she knew she'd bark a million questions at him. With her lips together, she thought to herself,

"How are we able to read each other's minds? Do your little fellas have some superhuman abilities that you infected me with when you came in my pussy?"

"No, not my sperm. At least I don't think so."

She gasped. "But we can really hear each other's thoughts?" She wasn't sure if that was a good thing because it meant she wasn't losing her mind... or a bad thing because it if it were true, she might rather be crazy because people would think it anyway.

"Among other things." He sighed. "Where's your father?"

"What in God's name does my dad have to do with this freak show?" She stood up and wrapped the sheet around herself. Jack might feel comfortable walking around naked, but she didn't.

"Just answer me, Lillian."

"He's at my grandma's, Jackson."

"Good grief, woman. When is he coming back?" Jack stalked over to her, and she held the sheet tightly to her chest.

"Couple weeks, I think. He didn't specifically say."

Jack nodded, stepped away from her,

and reached for his jeans. "Get dressed. We need to go."

"What makes you think I'm going anywhere with you, huh? First you're all lovey-dovey, then you freak out on me. I think I'll stay home today."

"You fucking work for me, Lillian. Get your pretty little butt dressed." Jack had managed to get almost completely dressed, and she was still wrapped in a sheet.

"I think I've done enough for you. Go to hell!"

He reached over and scooped her up. "What are you doing?" she yelled as he threw her over his shoulder in a fireman's carry.

"We have to go. Right now. I have to get you someplace safe before you decide you wanna attack me."

"Oh, I'm not gonna kick your ass. I'm gonna kill you, Jack!"

"That's what I'm afraid of," he mumbled as he carried her out of her bedroom. At least he'd left the sheet around her.

———

JACK POUNDED on Josh's door. He was

in some deep, deep trouble. Within the last twenty-four hours, he'd gone from just accepting a drink invitation with Lillian to mating with her.

And he wasn't dead.

Yet.

He remembered most of last night. It was quickly coming back to him. He'd gotten drunk while munching on chili. That crazy game she'd suggested as an ice-breaker had set the stage for them to fuck like animals.

And he'd bit her.

"Josh!" He pounded on the door again.

It swung open, and Josh stood there looking disheveled. "What?"

"We need to talk. Now."

"Too bad. I came by your place after breakfast, but you were gone. I've already worked several hours this morning, and Mikaela kept me up all night with her tossing and turning. She doesn't sleep. I don't sleep. I need a nap, dammit."

"It'll have to wait."

Jack grabbed his brother's arm and pulled him outside. Jack pulled the door shut just before he was yanked away from the house.

"Jesus, Jack. I need that arm."

Jack let go of him and kept on walking toward the trees.

"This is far enough, bro. Now what was able to wait last night but can't wait this morning?"

Jack turned around to face him, but stumbled back the last few steps so his body could collapse against the nearest tree.

"Not the same thing. That can wait. I fucked up, man. I fucked up big."

Josh's scowl eased away and was replaced with a look of concern. "Did something happen with Lillian?"

"You could say that."

"I did say that, Jack. What happened?"

"We got drunk." Smashed was more like it. "And had sex."

"Oookay. I take it that wasn't a good thing by how you're acting."

"Oh, the sex was off the charts from what I remember." Jack leaned over, resting his elbows above his knees.

"Then what's the problem? Do you think she didn't want to do it?"

"Oh, she wanted it. I'm beginning to think fucking me was her idea for the night anyway."

Jack knew he wasn't making much sense, but he was freaking out. And hungover. A bad combination for trying to think and speak clearly.

Josh shook his head. "What are you not telling me?"

Jack looked at his older brother. He couldn't say it. Not out loud. "*I mated with her.*"

"How?" Josh growled.

"I bit her while we were fucking, Josh. How do you think? Was it different for you and Mikaela, because that's the only way I know how to do it."

"Holy shit, Jack. How did you manage to get away from her?"

Jack laughed humorlessly as he stood up. "We were hammered. I'm surprised I was able to even get it up much less fight after. The details are sketchy, but I was still half buried in her when I woke up early this morning. I was still either too drunk or too hungover to register much more than that, so I pulled out, snuggled against her, and went right back to sleep. Based on that, I think we passed out right after."

Josh nodded. "Okay. So how did she

take the news? Apparently not too bad. You're still walking."

"She doesn't know."

"Hooo! That's rich." Josh chuckled. "You can't keep something like this from her. She's your mate."

"That's a fucking technicality!"

"One you have to live with, I'm afraid. Assuming she doesn't attack your ass as soon as you tell her."

"I can't think about that right now." Jack shook his head as he kicked at the leaves on the ground. This was a cluster-fuck of epic proportions.

"You have to, you know. You have to tell her. She can't go back home until she understands, and she can't live here and be surrounded by secrets. She has to know the truth. She's a part of this life now whether you like it or not."

"I know. I know. God, I know. I just can't believe I did something so fucking careless. Why didn't Ariel's meds stop me from claiming her?"

Josh shrugged. "You didn't attack her. Maybe the alcohol limited the effects of the medication or you were both too inebriated to be responsible about anything. You're a walking PSA, my man."

"Shut up," Jack said through gritted teeth.

Josh's chuckle died as he stepped closer to Jack. He clapped his brother on his shoulder. "Why you were able to claim her doesn't matter now. You need to focus on making this right. However you can."

Jack sighed. "I have to go talk to her."

"Where is she?"

"My cabin. I couldn't leave her at her dad's place. Not until she understands what's going on."

"You should get back to her, then, before she decides she doesn't want to stick around."

She'd made that decision before he'd even forced her to come over, but he wasn't telling Josh that. Once Jack had convinced her to take a nice long shower and relax, he'd locked her in. She wasn't going anywhere, and he couldn't allow her to leave until she accepted things. Shit, he didn't even know if *he* could accept things.

"Yeah, I know. At least her father is out of town right now. She won't be missed."

"Good. Then I think I should go tell

the family what's going on. I suspect you'll have your hands full with her for a while, and they need to be prepared for anything she might do."

"Okay. Thanks."

Josh chuckled as he stepped away from Jack. "Don't thank me yet, bro. Save that for when I'm blocking her attacks against you."

Jack paled. His brother was right. He'd be lucky to survive the night.

I'm in such deep shit.

CHAPTER FOUR

WAS THE MAN PART MOSQUITO? Her neck looked as though he'd fed from her for hours and hours.

She'd stared at it for a long time after her shower. The tee Jack had given her came down to her knees, but her neck was still exposed. She palpated it, watched the bruised skin turn white under her touch before the color rushed back into it, turning it an angry purple.

Or was he a vampire? He had bitten her neck. Maybe that was why they could read each other's thoughts. Could he turn into a bat, too? Eww! Surely he didn't turn into a flying rodent.

She was being crazy. There were no

such things as life-size mosquitoes or vampires of any kind.

Maybe he knew some sort of mind voodoo that enabled him to read her thoughts.

Oh, maybe he was a witch! *Hmm... warlock?* Were male witches called witches, or was that the female term? She'd have to Google that later. She left the bathroom and looked around the small cabin.

Not much was here. Maybe he didn't need many amenities to survive. She opened the fridge to find nothing in there either.

What if Jack and his family were blood-sucking aliens? Did people food make him sick? Had he eaten her chili last night? She couldn't remember. If they were aliens, did they need to buy her family's land for room to build a new mother ship to fly back home?

No. No. No. They'd lived there for as long as she could remember.

But maybe time was different for aliens.

She huffed as she stomped over to the bed to sit. She wasn't getting anywhere.

Her thoughts were so jumbled that nothing made sense.

The door rattled, and her heart raced.

She could hear little Caroline whisper, *They're here*, in the back of her head. But this wasn't the movie *Poltergeist*.

Hmm... could they be some kind of ghosts? She hadn't considered that one yet. Ghosts that lived in corporeal form. Maybe they were tree ghosts that cohabitated—

"Hey, I'm back," Jack said, cutting off her wayward thoughts.

"Oh, goodie."

He walked up to her and sighed. "I'm sorry I took you out of your house and left you here. There are some things we need to discuss."

"I gathered that."

He sat down beside her, and she jumped up, taking several steps back. "Hold up there. You have some splainin' to do, Lucy, and I'd prefer you stay ten feet from me until you do just that."

"That's probably not a bad idea," he mumbled.

Why was he agreeing with her? Was this some kind of trick?

"Do you remember when I said I

wanted to bite you while we were fuu—er, having sex?"

Really? She had the serpent's bite mark to prove it. She rolled her eyes and nodded.

"Well, I shouldn't have done that. Biting you bound you to me for all eternity since you are unmated."

"Er, come again? Please define the words *bound* and *eternity*."

He stood and started unbuttoning his shirt. "I'll just have to show you."

"Freeze, Batman. You aren't showing me a damn thing. I saw plenty last night."

He frowned, but dropped his hands. "Fine. When I bit you, I took you as my mate. It was an accident, I assure you. But the damage is done. We are a family of mountain lion shifters. We have a feral need to mate with any available female, and the consequences for taking an unwilling woman are dire, deadly. But last night I claimed you."

She laughed. Hysterically. Tears streamed down her face. "Oh, that's good, Count Dracula. You didn't claim a damn thing last night. And if you did and it was sooo deadly, then why are you still breathing?"

"Ariel had developed a drug to help with the lethal aggression. The need is still always there, but the drugs were supposed to help suppress it enough to avoid taking a woman unwillingly. If I hadn't been taking the medication, I wouldn't have been able to be around you at all."

"But you just said you took me last night? So you're not making any sense whatsoever. But nice try, space boy. Time for someone to beam you up and out of here."

He roared, and the blood drained from her face. That was a totally animalistic sound.

"Fuck it. I'll just ruin my clothes."

In the next instant, sounds of ripping material rent the air, and Lillian was staring at a cougar right where Jack had been standing. She'd watched as he literally morphed before her eyes.

"No," she breathed, her brain refusing to work.

"*Yes, Lilly.*"

"Lill*ian.*"

He growled. "You are so fucking stubborn. Here I am telling you about my life—

about your life—and you're seriously bitching at me about your name?"

"Guess this explains the whole mind-reading trick."

"It's speaking telepathically. My family and I can all do it. Mikaela and Krista can, too, since they are mated to my brothers."

"And you think I can do this because you and I are mated?" "Well, you're doing it, aren't you?"

The little prick had a point.

He shifted back into all his naked glory. "I have to admit, you're taking this better than I expected."

"So you're a freak of nature. Not my fucking problem. Have a nice life, kitty. Oh, and I quit."

She turned. She was getting the heck out of Dodge while the getting was good. From what she remembered of last night, the sex had rocked her, but if she had to face the unexplainable, then she'd rather be with someone like David.

"Whoever the fuck David is, you can forget it," Jack barked behind her.

She gasped and whirled. "Stay out of my head, Houdini."

"You're practically screaming it at me, Lilli*an*."

"So what, Jack*son*? This doesn't have anything to do with me. Go back to your catnip and mouse toys, and I'll pretend this never happened."

He growled and headed toward her. She started shaking. Maybe it wasn't a good idea to antagonize the beast. She needed to just make nice and get away.

"Sweet, sweet, Lilly. You seem to misunderstand. This is your life, too. Once I bit you, I made you a part of it. Welcome home, honey."

"Oh, hell to the no. You don't own me. It was just sex!" Okay, so making nice wasn't her forte.

"Only it wasn't, darlin'. Remember the noise you made when I snuggled up against you this morning?"

He took her wrist into his hand and put her palm against his face. Under his ministrations, she stroked his cheek, and that odd gurgling sound bubbled up from somewhere deep within him. It was similar to what she'd done this morning, but much deeper.

"What are you doing?" She barely

breathed out the words because she had a sinking feeling she knew. She just couldn't say it.

"I think you know." He shut his eyes as he leaned into her hand, rubbing his cheek against her. The noise got louder.

If she wasn't so freaked out, she might actually get turned on by being this close to him, but her brain could barely process what this meant to her, much less anything else.

He lifted his head and looked into her eyes. His blue eyes held a sense of sympathy and something else. Resolve?

"I was purring. Just like you did this morning."

"No! I'm not like you." She tried to back away from him, but Jack grabbed her hips and held her.

"You are now. You are mine. I will try to make this as easy for you as I can, but you need to start accepting it. We have no other choice."

She felt an odd sense of rage build within her. Anger, hurt, betrayal. Her senses were swimming in a sea of red. Her body hummed with an instinct to protect herself from this male, this man, who'd changed her. No! This man who was spilling lies to her.

She threw her head back and roared.

Jack jumped back, arms spread out in a defensive maneuver. As if that'd stop her from tearing him apart, the fool.

The tingles in her body got stronger, as though electrical currents were zinging all around her. Then her point of view changed. She'd had her head tilted up to stare into Jack's eyes, but now she was looking at his thighs. What the hell? A hiss fell from her mouth, and she choked it back. She looked down and saw tan-covered paws.

"No, no, no, no, no, no. This can't be happening."

"It is, Lilly. Let me help you. Please stay calm. We will get you through this," Jack's voice whispered through her mind. He took several steps back toward the fridge in the open space.

"You bastard! You infected me with some kind of kitty disease. No wonder my father never liked you all, you worthless troll!"

"You can call me all the names in the book, but it doesn't change things."

She growled and charged him. He jumped to the fridge. At least the loser knew better than to fight back. *"Run, little boy. I'll just kill you when I catch you."*

She caught up with him at the refrigerator and jumped, but Jack shoved his arm down her throat as she tried to rip it off. With his other hand, he yanked open the fridge and pulled something out. She barely saw the needle before she felt the sharp pain in her neck.

Lillian growled at him. *"What was that?"* But her mind was already getting foggy.

Jack panted as she slumped to the floor in front of him, releasing his arm. "An insurance policy. Ariel wanted us to have tranquilizers around the estate after my little aggressive mishap." He took in a lungful of air as he wiped the sweat from his brow. "When you wake up, I'll introduce you to her and the rest of your new family. Maybe we can talk them into throwing you a bridal shower or something." He smirked.

She shifted back to her normal self, and the floor was cold against her naked skin. She couldn't even see him anymore. Her eyes were too heavy. The darkness slowly came over her.

"Will... kill... you... later."

"Night-night, Lilly."

"Lilli*annn*."

———

JACK HELD Lillian by the arm as he escorted her to dinner. She was pissed, and he couldn't blame her. He'd taken away her right to choose, and now she was stuck here. If it could be any different, he'd tell her, but there just wasn't any other alternative.

She'd awoken an hour ago, groaning and cussing at him about fighting dirty. He'd laid out something for her to wear, but she'd turned her nose up at it and grabbed something else out of the bag of Mikaela's clothes she had left for her. She'd bitched and growled at him the whole time she got ready, and each time Lillian's anger got to the breaking point, he'd wave another sedative in front of her. He didn't like the idea of keeping her drugged, but she was being difficult on purpose.

He'd finally explained to her that she

needed to stick around at least until she'd accepted what had happened and learned to deal with it, but she was still argumentative. The little minx would argue with the sky about its color if she thought she could get it to fight back. And when he thought he'd take the high road and not let her bait him, he'd instead swallow that bait and beg like a dog seeking a treat every damn time. He didn't know what it was about her that caused fire to stir within him. If it wasn't the heat of attraction, it was the blaze of infuriation. Either way, she burned him.

"There better be something good to eat here. I haven't eaten all day," she grumbled as she walked beside him.

"You've been asleep all day. Hard to eat when you're not awake."

"Hard to stay awake when you're being drugged."

Jack groaned as they rounded the corner and came up to the dining room door. He pushed it open, but this time, there was no laughter to die down, only soft murmurs that immediately ceased. He walked up to the table where everyone had gathered, knowing he wore a somber look on his face.

The feeling was too deeply ingrained to hide right now.

"I'd like you all to meet Lillian Caldwell."

"We met her yesterday when you were showing her around," Rob said softly to him and then looked at Lillian. "It's nice to see you again."

"Hmph." She looked away, not meeting anybody's stares.

Jack sighed. "Right. Um, Lilly, this is Krista, Ariel, and Mikaela."

Her eyes cut to him. "Lill*ian*." Then she looked at the women. "Are you all prisoners of the cat people, too? I say we rise against them and break free."

Mikaela frowned at her. "You're part of this family now, too. We're all alike."

"Oh, right." Lillian turned to Jack with mock excitement. "Hey, love muffin, can we get T-shirts that say Thing One and Thing Two? You get to be number two, shit ball."

Toby busted out laughing. "I'm gonna like her."

Krista elbowed him, but Toby wasn't the only one who found Jack's miserable life humorous. Josh and Rob both had their mouths pressed in thin lines, but the dancing in their eyes and the slight shaking of their shoulders gave away their need to join Toby.

Thomas cleared his throat. "Jeffery has already set the table. We felt it'd be best to have dinner already waiting."

Mikaela smiled. "What he's really saying is that he's quickly learned not to keep the pregnant woman waiting for food."

She turned and headed to the other side of the table. Josh stayed on this side, and Mikaela took the seat across from him. Rob left a seat empty next to Josh. Ariel sat across from her mate. Krista sat next to Ariel, and Toby sat next to Rob. So the women were all sitting across from the men, leaving a spot for Jack and Lillian to sit next to Josh and Mikaela.

Jack walked Lillian around the table, and she huffed as she fell onto her chair. He tried pushing her up to the table once she'd seated herself, but she whipped her head around and glared at him. He lifted his hands in surrender and walked to his seat.

Everybody passed food around, and he

kept glancing up to watch her. She took a little bit of everything, but he wasn't sure if it was because she was really hungry or if she was just being polite, though that was *not* a word he'd typically use to describe her.

"So, Josh, how did things go today on the northern side of the estate?" Thomas asked as he cut his brisket.

Josh's eyes slid to Mikaela before he picked up his fork and answered, "Good, good. Should finish up in a couple of weeks."

Jack looked at Mikaela. She was scarfing down her diner. Then he looked at the other women. They were still fixing their plates. His other brothers sat patiently by, waiting. He groaned. He'd forgotten about the need for a male to let his mate start eating before he ate. It was something that had been ingrained in them, but not something Jack had to experience before.

Until now.

He looked at his fork and picked it up. Maybe he wouldn't have to wait. It wasn't as though he was in love with her or any-thing. As he held his fork, he felt sweat bead his brow as a nauseous feeling engulfed him. As the seconds ticked by, the feeling got so strong that he'd start dry heaving at any moment. He slammed his fork down. "Shit!"

"Don't worry, bro," Rob said. "You'll get used to it."

As if that was supposed to make him feel better.

Lillian tilted her head to the side, watching him. She'd already picked up her fork, but Jack's little outburst had startled her. "Get used to what?"

Ariel leaned over and whispered, "He can't start eating until you do. It's something about the mating bond." She shrugged, then scooped up some potatoes and took a bite.

Lillian chuckled, looking at him now. Hell, that didn't sound good.

"You mean you can't eat until I do?"

"That's what she just said, wasn't it?"

Lillian dropped her fork and crossed her arms. "Oh, I'm not hungry."

Jack growled. "You just said you were starving not ten minutes ago."

"It's passed."

"You're fucking lying, Lilly. Quit being childish and eat."

"Lilli*an*. And I think I have every right to be however the hell I want to be after you did this to me."

"Why do you have to be so difficult? Just pick up your fork and eat, for Christ's sake."

"Jack." Thomas's low voice didn't distract either of them.

"You can't tell me what to do, Garfield. I don't have to eat if I don't want to."

"You'll starve, Lilli*an*."

"So will you, Jack*son*."

"Lillian, please." Thomas tried again, this time with her and not Jack. "I apologize for what has happened. I know this has to be incredibly difficult, but if we're going to figure this out, we need to stay focused. And strong." He looked pointedly at her plate.

She sighed, looked at her plate, and picked up her fork. "Can you only eat what I eat?" she asked Jack with an eyebrow raised.

"I can eat whatever I want as soon as you start to eat."

"Too bad. Would've been fun killing you by making you eat something you're allergic to, sugar booger."

She took her first bite, and Jack felt the tension ease from his shoulders as he glanced around the room. His brothers, *all* his brothers, had smiles plastered on their faces.

God, what a mess.

CHAPTER FIVE

"REMEMBER, you have to do exactly as I say."

Lillian glared at Jack as they stood in the woods. She was tired of his damn orders. She wasn't a toddler. Just because Jack pissed her off didn't mean she didn't know how to follow directions. She just wanted to reserve the right *not* to follow said directions.

Eating with his family hadn't been too horrible, though she didn't really care to carry on any major conversations. She'd heard them all hypothesizing about how she hadn't attacked Jack after the mating. Yeah, that was a new experience. Never had her sex life been a topic for dinner conversation. At least the chatter had never veered into positions or technique used. That would've definitely been cringe-worthy. But Thomas had seemed genuinely concerned that an attack could still happen. Josh believed the worst of the danger had passed. The others hadn't known what to think about it, and they'd all agreed that Jack should stay armed with a sedative in case she got her panties in a wad over something.

Just what she needed, a pissed-off kitty armed with a needle.

After dinner, her newfound lover had decided she should run with him in cat form, said some crap about it helping her adjust to her new way of life. She'd refused at first, but he'd been determined. She'd threatened to neuter him, and he'd spouted off something about her just trying to find an excuse to touch his balls. She would find his relentlessness funny if it wasn't about her, so it just made her even madder at him instead.

"Yes, yes, my liege." She twirled her arm and bowed. "Stay at your flank. Don't run off. We're only running to the border of our properties and back. Don't run off. Don't attack the animals. Don't run off.

Don't attack you. Don't run off. I think I got it. Though I'm not clear on the whole *running off* rule. Do you mean no running off something like a cliff or no running off in general?" She smirked.

"Both."

Lillian nodded as she headed away from him, but he grabbed her arm and whirled her around.

"Where do you think you're going?"

"To put on my cat costume, Simba." She paused, her eyes popping open wider. "You think I'd let you see me naked, honey bear? Tsk, tsk, tsk. That's what you get for thinking, big guy." She yanked her arm free.

"Don't go far."

"Fuck off."

He growled, but didn't come after her. She walked a few feet into the forest, where she felt she was covered from Jack's prying eyes. It was ironic how just a couple of days' time had changed things.

This time yesterday they had been either getting plastered or already having sex. And tonight they were going to go running in the woods, maybe find a spider or two to play with until it died or played dead. *You sure know how to pick 'em, Lillian.*

She stripped out of her borrowed clothing and shifted. Changing into an animal seemed much easier this second time. It still felt odd, but not uncomfortable. Hopefully it would continue to become easier.

Ugh, easier? Why was she concerned with making this easier? Her infector never said shifting was mandatory, so maybe she wouldn't have to do it ever again once she left this place. She could try to live a normal life sans Jack and this mountain-lion mumbo jumbo. Maybe if she ignored it long enough, she could pretend to be normal again.

And Jack was another matter entirely. Her feelings were confused. There was no denying some kind of connection with him —at least to herself. She could and would deny it with him. Plus, she still wanted to hurt him in the worst way, but she tried really hard not to dwell on those emotions. The initial urge to kill him was slowly getting better.

Because death would be too easy.

If she had to live life as a freak, then he

should be forced to live in pain and suffering, too.

"Ready or not, here I come," she thought as she trotted out to where Jack had been. Now he was in his mountain-lion form, too.

"I know what you look like when you come, and this isn't it."

"You're an ass."

"Follow me."

For what felt like hours, they ran. They'd made it to the property line and back several times, zigzagging throughout the trees, stopping to sip at the creeks, and even chasing a field mouse once.

For the first time in her life, Lillian felt alive. Free. As the wind ruffled her short fur, she felt as if she could spread her legs and fly.

They hadn't spoken much, and she was okay with that. If the jerk opened his mind up to her, she just knew it would ruin the peacefulness of this experience. But that also left her alone with her confused thoughts about this ability and way of life. Why was she so accepting of it? *Because for the first time in a long time, you feel cherished.* That thought shocked her. Her mother had always nurtured her, but after the accident that had taken her from Lillian, she'd been left with her father as the sole provider of all things. His love had been lacking, but he worked hard to provide for them, so she had no right to complain.

But why did she feel cherished now? It wasn't as though Jack was gushing all over her. He was still a prick.

When they reached the gate that led to her property from his, Jack slowed.

"*This gate was left open yesterday, too. I think Rob is working this section. I'll need to remind him to lock it when he's done.*"

"*This is the way I came yesterday to work. Maybe he left it open because he thought I'd be using this path to get to and from work.*"

"*No. He knew earlier today that you wouldn't be going back home. He should've locked it before dinner.*"

She growled at him. "*So after you drugged me, you ran and bragged to your family about kidnapping me. Do you think this gate will hold me here?*" If this was what she thought feeling cherished meant, then she needed to seek a psychiatrist, like, yesterday. Her father's lack of love must've really done a number on her.

He hissed at her. "You know it wasn't like that. But I did inform them of what had happened. And no, I don't think this gate will keep you here, but it needs to stay locked."

"Because?"

"Because I fucking said so!"

That was it. She lunged for him, snapping at his throat. She'd had all she could stand of his righteous attitude. She was pissed at him, and at herself, for him making her feel so confused. He rolled them, pinning her beneath him. She tried wiggling out from under him as she growled and hissed, but all she managed to do was get herself off her back, onto her legs. Things had just gone from bad to worse because now he straddled her backside in a stance of complete control.

And it felt right.

His teeth scraped against the scruff of her neck and bit. He was too powerful to resist. Somewhere deep inside she knew it was her place to submit to him, and when she felt his erection against her tail, she couldn't help the needy sound that slipped out or the head that bowed and rested on the ground. She didn't want this. She. Did. Not. Want. This. But need... now *that* was clawing at her.

"*Shift.*"

It was a command she couldn't ignore. Her traitorous body was aching for him, for whatever he wanted. She didn't know if this was tied to the bonding thing or the fact that she just needed to feel him inside her. She shifted, and in that same moment, she sensed him shifting, too.

His palms cupped her hips and lifted her until she was on her hands and knees. Then he wrapped one arm around her belly and used the other hand to grab his cock. He rubbed it against her soaked slit, and she leaned her head against his shoulder and moaned.

"So wet, Lilly. You want me to fuck you just as bad as I want to take you, don't you?"

She moaned. God, he was right, but she wasn't going to tell him that.

He growled behind her at her refusal to admit the truth and plunged into her with one hard thrust.

She screamed and bucked against him,

her sensitive tissues flaring to life. He bit her neck as he pounded into her.

"You'll fucking say it," he demanded.

"No," she breathed. She couldn't. She wouldn't.

He pushed her shoulders down to the ground, forcing her ass up in the air, and fucked her harder. She panted, her orgasm building so fast she was already lost. Her pussy convulsed. Her spine tingled.

She was so close she knew she was about to go over, and she didn't care. She wanted it. She needed it. She needed Jack to give it to her.

He stopped and pulled out, still holding her down. She was empty, lonely, aching. She felt wetness hit her back and realized he was sweating with the effort to either hold her in place or hold back his own release.

"Say it, Lilly."

Oh God, he wasn't going to let her come. He was going to torture them both until he got what he wanted.

"You're the devil! Just fuck me."

"Say it."

She groaned and tried rubbing her ass

against his erection to entice him back into the warmth of her velvet heat.

"I will masturbate and use my seed to mark your back if you don't tell me the truth right now, damn you!"

"Yes! Yes, I want you to fuck me. I want you to take me. To own me. To—"

He knifed into her, and she screamed.

"God, I want you so bad, Lilly."

She wanted him too, and she knew she was going to hate herself for it. She was at her body's mercy. Maybe it was the lack of sex or how strong and sexy Jack was, but right now, she just needed this.

And so she gave herself over to it. She grabbed handfuls of grass and arched her back as much as she could, allowing him to take her as deeply as he could. Each time he pushed into her, he hit her cervix and she whimpered, "So good."

She came on a sobbing scream, and seconds later, Jack roared behind her, his cock jerking inside her with each spurt of his release. Never had she let a man take her bare before Jack, yet the thought of him allowing a condom between them felt unacceptable to her now.

That sobered her. No! She was not

some whiny little tart. She stiffened, and she heard and felt Jack's sigh against her shoulder.

He eased out and away from her, and Lillian scrambled to her feet. She looked at him and growled.

"Stay the hell away from me."

She shifted back into the abomination that was her new alter ego and ran.

———

JACK COULDN'T EXPLAIN what had come over him when he'd been in the woods with Lillian. He'd been determined to teach her about hunting and expose her to the new aspect of her life, but the moment she'd come out as a mountain lion, all he could think was *mate*. It was hard to argue with her at times, but while in his feral form, he just wanted to dominate her.

So he'd kept his mouth shut and just focused on the tasks. He'd run them all over the place in hopes that the need to take her would ease. He wasn't that lucky. It was always there, taunting him. He'd barely held it at bay up until she'd charged him. His lion had taken control at that point, and he'd been helpless to stop it. He'd just been thankful he'd mustered enough willpower to shift back into his manly form. Taking her as a lion would've been too personal. That was reserved for mates, mates who wanted to conceive.

After they'd had sex, Lillian had run. He couldn't blame her. He felt the same need to flee. But the need to stay and make her understand was slowly taking over that desire to stay away from her. So he'd forced himself not to follow her. She'd headed back toward the direction of the cabins and not her father's house, so there wasn't an immediate concern she'd escape the estate. No reason to make her understand he was just as tormented as she was. All the reasons weren't the same, but the struggles were there.

When he'd gotten back to his cabin, he was pleased to smell her scent was strong there. She was home. She'd run from him, but she'd run back to his cabin. She could've sought refuge at the main house or with one of the other ladies, but she hadn't. Jack had tried not to feel the pride swell up at her choice, but the feelings had bubbled up anyway. When he'd gone inside, he'd found her asleep on the bed. She'd put on one of his T-shirts and was huddled in the corner, but she'd been there.

He'd showered, slipped on some boxers, and slid into bed beside her, trying not to touch her. His body was so large that there wasn't much space between them, but he didn't want to disturb her while he slept.

But sleep had eluded him most of the night. He'd have tossed and turned more if he hadn't been worried about waking her. He did sleep in fits, but by dawn, he'd accepted it as a lost cause.

He gently sat up and pulled open his nightstand drawer to retrieve the photo of his mother. Just a few days ago, this had been the dominating factor of his mind. Now it was just a nagging thought on the sidelines. Granted, his life had changed drastically, but his family history shouldn't be ignored.

He needed to talk to Josh about what he'd discovered and the theories it raised. If he was right, his father wasn't the reason for their existence, as they'd all been led to believe. It had been his mother all along.

"What's that?" Lillian asked, her voice roughened with sleep.

Jack tossed the photo back into the drawer and shut it. He couldn't share this with her. Not now. Not yet. "Nothing."

He looked over his shoulder and stopped breathing. She was truly beautiful, her blonde hair mussed, her big blue eyes soft. She held the blanket against her chest and yawned. So innocent-looking.

"I'm surprised you came back here last night. I figured you'd run to one of the women."

She huffed. "Why would I run to one of the Stepford wives? Sorry, but no, 'I don't *want* to squeeze the goddamn Charmin,'" she said in a singsong voice.

"What the hell does that mean?"

"It's from the movie. *Stepford Wives*? I don't want to squeeze—" She sighed. "Never mind. Point is, they seem a little too accepting of this way of life, and I have no intentions of being brainwashed into a mindless zombie homemaker of the cat people."

He'd really thought her innocent? Maybe in looks, but her spirit was full of spunk. "They are not mindless women. There are here because they want to be."

"So they got a choice, but I didn't. How's that fair, Felix?"

He chuckled. "You'll run out of cat names eventually." Then he shook his head. "It's not fair. I never said it was. We got drunk and mated. I'm going through this just as blindly as you are."

She pushed the blanket off and shuffled to her feet. "Not true. I didn't turn you into a freak of nature."

Jack stood, too, his hands fisting at his sides. "I'm getting really sick and tired of you fighting with me at every possibility. I didn't mean for this to happen. Hell, I didn't even want to get drinks with you that night anyway. You were the stubborn one who wouldn't take no for a fucking answer!"

She recoiled as if he'd physically slapped her, and the sudden pang of sadness he felt at causing her any kind of harm almost knocked the breath out of him. "God, I'm sorry." He moved toward her, but she shook her head, looking away from him, her defenses down. Seeing the wounded look in her eyes was killing him. "Lilly."

She jerked, fire blazing in her eyes again. "How many times do I have to say it's Lill*ian*?"

He hadn't intended to rouse her by using the pet name he had for her. But, yes. He'd rather have her fighting mad than unhappy. Maybe he could keep her distracted with this train of thought, but he'd be lying if he didn't acknowledge that her resistance to her nickname had raised suspicions that he would like cleared up.

"Why are you so determined to keep me from calling you Lilly?"

"Because that's not my name," she gritted out.

He smirked. "Well, my name isn't Felix or Simba or Garfield or any of the other names you've used to call me the last couple of days."

She smiled. "True, but I like calling you those names."

"And I like calling you Lilly, Lilly."

Lillian narrowed her eyes. Her hands poised at her hips. "Fine, you win. Call me whatever you want. It doesn't matter to me anyway, Heathcliff."

His cock jerked. God, that feistiness was going to be the death of him. Jack couldn't seem to ignore it, or his body, as well as he had yesterday.

She turned, and he grabbed her arm and hauled her against him. "What if I call you mine?" he growled in her ear.

She gasped, and he could feel the tremble coursing through her. "I am not going let you seduce me whenever you please, Jack." But she didn't sound convincing, and from her stance, he knew she hadn't believed those words either.

"Tell me to stop." Part of him hoped she would. Not because he didn't want her, but because if she resisted, he could blame his growing need for her on his feral side. The lion wouldn't take her resistance lying down. It'd roar to the surface and show her how much she wanted him.

But if she stayed pliable, he wouldn't have anyone, anything to blame but himself if he took her.

"I—Jack," she breathed as she melted against him. "Why is it so hard to push you away when you're this close?" She'd said it so softly, he couldn't be sure she was actually talking to him or to herself.

"Our lions recognize the mate in the other," he rasped as he took her lobe into his mouth and nibbled.

"So you're not—" she started, but hesitated, and Jack didn't give her an opportunity to finish. He pushed her up against the nearest wall and pulled down her panties as he squatted behind her.

He spread her cheeks apart, burrowed his face between her legs, and inhaled. "I love the way you smell," he groaned. Then his tongue peeked out and licked the backside of her pussy.

Lillian gasped, lifted up on her toes, and arched her back to provide better access.

He tried savoring her taste, sweet with a unique flavor all her own, but he was starving for her. He nibbled her labia before shoving his tongue inside her. Lillian moaned and rocked against him, so he gripped her tighter to keep her still. He was going to feast on her and make her come so hard that he feared he'd spill inside his boxers.

He groaned when her pussy started contracting around his invasion, her honey leaking onto his tongue. So fucking sweet.

He could get drunk off her. When he pulled his tongue out, she whimpered. Oh, he wasn't stopping. It'd take an act of God for him to quit, and even then, he'd still resist. His tongue circled her clit, and he drew it into his mouth at the same time he pushed two fingers into her.

Lillian screamed, her pussy fisting around his fingers so tightly that his dick ached even more to be inside her. He pushed his boxers down as he stood up and pulled his fingers out. Within seconds, he had the throbbing head of his cock rubbing against her entrance. He pushed in on a groan, her body milking him, needing him, as she screeched and lifted higher on her toes.

"You're not going anywhere, Lilly," he panted as he took her with punishing thrusts. "You're mine, and I'll have you whenever and however I want."

"You're a pig." But she rotated her hips to meet his taking.

"I'm a predator." And he knew in that moment, he would never be able to let her go. He'd hunt her down if she ever tried to leave. That thought didn't make him happy. At all. He groaned as he shoved into her harder, punishing himself for wanting her as much as he was punishing her for not stopping him.

She screamed, and her juices flooded him as she came. The feel of her coming loose around him threw him over the edge too. He roared as he slammed into her so hard he pushed her completely up against the wall. His hips kept pumping, taking, as if he could do nothing but lose himself to the feel of being inside her, owning her. His mate.

With the final jerk of his cock, Jack slumped against her as he tried taking in a deep breath. The sweat between them chilled his skin, so he gently stood up and eased out of her. He walked to the bathroom without looking at her, worried he'd still see hurt or anger in her eyes. He barely knew how to handle her when she was her normal, feisty self. He wasn't ready to face any more backlashes for what he'd done to her. Jack washed off at the sink and wetted a cloth so he could now tend to her, a reaction that felt completely natural to him. When he stepped out, however, she was waiting at the door with her arms crossed.

"Took you long enough." She pushed past him and slammed the door shut.

Jack just stared down at the washcloth and gritted his teeth. His mate really knew how to push his buttons, and Jack wondered if this was Karma's way of getting back at him for his general attitude toward taking a mate up until he'd found her.

If so, Karma was a bitch.

CHAPTER SIX

LILLIAN WALKED to the main house after ditching Jack in the woods yet again. This had been her morning ritual for almost a week now. Ever since he'd taken her against the wall, she knew she wouldn't be able to deny whatever he wanted. That morning, her defenses had been down. She'd been vocal about wondering why she was drawn to him and he'd been so callous as to say it was because his lion recognized his mate.

As if she could be fat and covered with warts and it wouldn't matter.

More importantly, that there were no affectionate feelings on his part. When she'd seen him holding some photo and saw the longing in his eyes, she felt her armor crack. *Maybe I can grow to love him.* But that thought was quickly squashed by his cold treatment of her. She was a warm body to him.

Nothing more.

And she was trapped here, spending her days working in the tree fields and her nights and mornings having sex with Jack.

The sex had been good. He was very methodical and take-charge about it, but what had started out as hot and heavy, just became an itch that needed scratching. If she didn't get away from here, she feared that she would really lose her heart to him and he'd crush it with his bare paws.

She'd also been avoiding his family. A mistake, she now realized, because if she wanted to break free, she would probably need to form some allies. She could try appealing to Jack's father's sense of remorse, but Lillian felt the end result could go either way with him. What if he were to side with his son? No, she needed girl power on her side, which was why this morning she was headed somewhere very specific at the main house.

The office where Mikaela and Krista worked.

She rounded the corner and came up to

the cracked door. She lifted her hand to knock, but then hesitated. Girlie chitchat was never her style. What if these were the types of women who'd stab her in the back?

"You gonna stand out there all morning?" Mikaela called out. "We can see you peeking through the door."

Damn. Lillian took a deep breath and stepped through. "Hi."

"We were wondering if you were ever going to come talk to us," Krista said, putting down some wickedly thick book that probably consisted of legal jargon.

Lillian walked over to the ladies and leaned against the desk. "Um, yeah, I've been a little angry."

Mikaela chuckled while rubbing her pregnant belly. "That's one way to put it. Girl, you have Jack all tied up in knots. It's actually quite refreshing to see him like this."

"Refreshing, huh? Well, I'm still mad about what Jack did to me, but I figured I shouldn't punish everybody else because of what he did." Lillian shrugged. "Besides, I don't want to stay cooped up here forever."

Mikaela half smiled at her. "It's really

not like that, Lillian. If you want to go home, you can."

Lillian frowned. "That's easy for you to say. You don't have a big man demanding you not leave this estate."

"Oh, we had our own men trying to call the shots. They might wear the pants in the family, but we wear the panties." She smiled brightly. "God, I love being a woman."

Krista stood and walked around the desk. "I left before Toby and I mated. I was in love with him, but I couldn't be sure if he was what I wanted."

Lillian gaped at her. "And he let you leave? Just like that?"

Krista nodded. "Just like that."

"You weren't mated, though, Krista. Could you image living away from Toby now?" Mikaela asked.

"Well, no, but I think deep down our men will live a life of misery if they thought it made us happy to be away from here." She turned to Lillian. "If you really wanted to go, whether for the day or forever, Jack would let you."

"Of course, you'd have to promise not to tell our little family secret," Mikaela said.

This was Lillian's opportunity, her way out. She'd cast the bait and hooked her fish. Now she needed to reel them in. "And you'd help me? Talk to him, I mean?"

"Absolutely," Mikaela said. "He only needed you here to help show you that you weren't a freak of nature and make sure you understood this new part of your life. Even if you don't stay with Jack, you'll never be the same again. It would have been careless of him to just let you go around not under-standing."

Lillian tried not to roll her eyes. "I think he kept me around to sate his carnal hunger, not show me the ropes."

Krista's eyes narrowed. "Did he force himself on you?"

Her cold tone made Lillian shift into defensive mode. "Hell no. I know how to take care of myself."

"I'm sorry. There was an incident with him and my sister when she was trying to medicate him and Rob."

Mikaela nodded solemnly. "Yeah, Jack hadn't been taking his meds and tried to rape her."

"He hadn't been taking his shots like he

should've been, so he was a danger to her. He should've known better."

Lillian's hackles rose at Krista's snippy remark. She leveled Krista with a flat stare. "He told me he attacked her. And he apologized. She doesn't seem too scared of him when I've seen her around. Maybe you should let it go." There went her idea of making friends. But Krista's snarky attitude just pissed her off. If anybody was going to be mad at Jack, it was going to be Lillian. Period. End of discussion.

She turned to leave, but felt a hand grab her arm. She turned around and saw Mikaela holding on to her. "Krista loves her sister. That was a very hard situation for everyone. But I think you're good for Jack. You obviously care enough about him to defend him."

Lillian pulled her arm free. She didn't need girlfriends to speak her case to Jack about leaving. She was insane for even trying to make friends with them. "I'm going home. It was nice meeting you all. Have a nice life."

She could not care about Jack. She wouldn't. And she was damn tired of wearing other people's clothes and brushing with a cheap toothbrush. She wanted her own clothes, toiletries, and bed. Besides, her father would be back soon, and she needed to clean out the fridge and do some laundry.

She had a life back home, and it was time she got back to living it.

———

JACK CAME BARRELING up to the dining room door just before dinner. He hadn't even showered and changed out of his work clothes, so he was still wearing dirty jeans and boots. Not that it mattered. He had one thing on his mind. He was going to paddle Lilly's ass! She hadn't returned to work at all that afternoon.

He'd come to expect her little disappearing act in midmornings and not seeing her again until early afternoon. Hell, he'd silently cheered when she would sneak away because it would give him time cool his growing hunger for her. If she really knew how much he wanted her, he'd be embarrassed.

He'd gone from needing her to wanting her.

He was okay with the idea of needing her. His body needed release, and his lion needed its mate.

But wanting her? No, that wasn't something he was looking forward to. Wanting her company, wanting her touch on him, wanting her snippy little voice bitching at him, he was a glutton for punishment when it came to Lillian Caldwell, and he couldn't help it. She pissed him off and turned him on, and he could not get enough of her.

Which was why he'd searched everywhere for her when she hadn't returned to work. He had yet to find her. But when he did...

Jack pushed the dining room door open amid the murmurs of his family and quickly scanned the room for his wayward mate, assuming she'd come out of her hidey-hole for dinner.

He'd assumed incorrectly. *Shit*. She wasn't in here either.

"Where is she?"

"Who?" Mikaela asked coyly.

Jack growled. "You fucking know who."

"You better back off, bro, or I'll take you out. You know better than to growl at my mate," Josh warned.

Jack shook his head and grunted. "Where. Is. Lillian?"

"She went home," Krista said. "She snapped at me and said she was leaving."

Mikaela sighed. "She was provoked, Krista," she said without any judgment. "You'd have acted the same if someone bad-mouthed Toby to you."

Ariel walked over to Jack, and damn if his shoulders didn't relax a little.

"Krista told me that the attack came up in conversation earlier." Jack winced, knowing what attack she was referring to, but Ariel continued. "She said that Lillian stood up for you and went home. Her intention was to go home anyway, and I think you should give her what she wants."

Jack felt his blood pressure rise. He knew he should give her what she wanted, but the thought of letting her go—

"But I think you need to talk to her first," Ariel said. "If she still wants to stay away, then let her, but don't just let her walk out. Not without at least thanking her for watching your back."

Lillian had stood up for him? To Krista? Jack was shocked past words. He couldn't remember anyone ever doing something like that for him before. Not that he'd deserved it where Ariel was concerned, but the fact that his Lilly had done so for him, well, it warmed something deep within his chest.

And he still wanted to spank her ass for running out.

"Yeah, I should go talk to her. Thanks." He turned to leave, not looking at anybody else.

Once he got outside, he jumped on his wheeler and headed straight for Lillian's house. When he reached the gate that separated their old property lines, he smiled as he stopped. Unless she went down his driveway, hit the main road, and then drove to her estate on the shoulder of the highway, the little minx must've swiped some keys since the gate was locked. And thinking she could keep him away, she'd locked it back. He killed the engine and grabbed his keys. He unlocked it, drove through, and locked it back before proceeding to her father's house. She'd need to do more than a locked gate to keep him away.

Jack slowed as he neared his destination. Lillian's four-wheeler was parked out front, and there were lights on in the house.

At least she wasn't trying to pretend she wasn't home. He parked his wheeler next to hers and walked to the door. He was still irritated that she'd run from him, but after learning that she'd also stood up for him, it made him feel other things he didn't even want to try to identify.

He knocked on the door, but didn't have to wait long. It flew open on the second knock.

"No animals allowed."

God, she was beautiful. Even with her hair all tied up in some crazy-looking knot, rubber gloves, and a ratty T-shirt on, and smelling like lemon-scented cleaner, she still took his breath away.

"Then what are you doing in there, *foxy* mama?"

She snorted, her hands dropping from the doorjamb. "Good one"—she glanced at his shoes—

"Puss in Boots."

He chuckled because he just couldn't help it. Her smile was contagious. "You know you really will run out of cat insults eventually."

She winked at him. "I've got a ton of them." Then she stepped back and motioned for him to come in. "You're letting all the heat out."

Jack walked in and turned to face her. "I think you know why I'm here."

Lillian sighed as she walked to the couch. The cabin was much bigger than it looked on the outside.

"Because I left."

Jack came over and sat next to her. At least she didn't jump up and away from him. "Why?"

She looked at him, really looked at him, and he felt naked. "Because I don't belong with you."

Her words were a sucker punch, but he schooled his expression, wanting her to continue.

"And you only want me because of the weird mating thing," she said quickly as she looked away.

Interesting. She almost looked hurt by what she'd said.

"What makes you think that, Lilly?"

She glared at him. "Because when I said I didn't understand why I was drawn to you, you quickly blamed the lion mating thing. It was as if you didn't care anything about me specifically."

Ah, hell. "I didn't know you."

"You still don't know me, Jack. Hell, I don't know you either. The one time I tried to talk to you, you shut me out. You just want me for sex and nothing more. The sex is good, but I need more than that from a man. Not that I expect you to be that man."

"When have I ever shut you out?" Hell, she was in his every waking thought.

She growled at him. "That morning you were looking at some photo. I could tell you were bothered by something, but when I tried to ask, you swatted me away like some pestering fly. I'm good enough to fuck, but not good enough to talk to."

The photo of his mother. He remembered not wanting to talk to her about it. It was too personal, the news of it changing everything he'd been raised to believe. Hell, he hadn't even talked to Josh about it yet, so how could he just open up to her about it?

Because you want to.

And as he watched her scanning the room, avoiding eye contact, he knew he was right. Even if it didn't change things with them, he still wanted to talk to her about that news. Somewhere deep within him, he needed her to know, and he wasn't going to fight that.

"It was a photo of my mom," he mumbled, looking down at his clasped hands in his lap. He saw her head turn toward him through the corner of his eye.

She sighed. "You don't have to do me any favors by telling me."

"I'm not, Lilly. This is just really hard for me to talk about."

She shifted on the couch, but didn't touch him. "How long ago did she die?"

"Not long. A few years." He was silent for several seconds, not knowing how to continue. Her death wasn't the issue now. It was her life. Finally, he rubbed his hands together, tilted his head to the side to look at Lillian, and found the strength he needed there. "My brothers and I were led to believe that we are mountain lion shifters because of my father's heritage, that his parents died when he was little, and the secret of our existence died with them."

She nodded slowly, seemingly taking it in and understanding what he'd really said. "Led to believe?"

"That's right. That photo of my mother, Lina Woods, changes that belief. In it, she was younger and standing with several people I don't recognize. I was in my father's office having a conference call with you when I stumbled upon it."

"What about that picture makes you question what you've been told about your parents?"

"The note on the back. God, I stared at it for so long that I remember it word for word. It read, 'To my sister, Felina, please remember the times like this when we were a happy family, and forgive my intrusion with your selection of Thomas as your mate. Your rightful place will always be as the queen of our people. We extend a welcoming hand to you and your chosen mate and hope you make the journey home to your throne.' It was signed 'Rodrick Lyons,' a name I'd never heard before."

"What?" Lillian shook her and frowned at him. "So there's a litter of you guys somewhere else? And your mom was their leader? Really?"

"Yeah, that's what I think. So my father, Thomas, isn't the reason we can shift into mountain lions. If this Rodrick guy is my mom's brother, and he said *her people*, that makes me think she's also the reason we can shift, the missing link. So why the cover-up? And what really happened to make my mom leave her people?"

"Hmm, that *is* interesting." Lilly leaned back against the couch and scratched her chin. "There has to be a serious reason why your parents never told you about her family. Did your dad explain anything when you told him what you'd found?"

Jack half smiled. "I haven't told him yet. I haven't told anyone. Until now."

Her brows shot up. "Why? What are you waiting for? This is about your life. You deserve to know the truth."

He lifted his hands in defense. God, she was always so feisty. "I agree. I wanted to get Josh's opinion on it before discussing it with my father, but the morning I was supposed to meet him, I was busy staring at a nasty bite mark on your neck and trying not to shit my britches."

Lillian chuckled. "I guess you did have your hands full."

"And have had them full pretty much ever since." He smiled at her.

She nodded. "Right."

Jack stared at her, words he should say, words he should not say swimming around in his head. He knew if he said the wrong thing, he'd regret it. He sensed she was balancing on some fence, and he didn't need to push her to the wrong side.

But what side was right?

Hell, he didn't know.

"Will you come with me while I talk to my family about this?" The words rushed out, as if he knew that was what he really wanted all along.

She smiled brightly. "You want me there with you?"

He leaned his forehead against hers and gently wrapped his fingers around her waist. "Yes. I want you there. I-I need you there."

Her sweet breath brushed against his cheek, and he bit back a groan. They'd been having sex twice a day, every day, and it still wasn't enough. But he needed to stay focused. The comment she'd made about not being good enough to talk to really struck him, and he didn't want her to think he wanted her only for sex.

She moved back and stared at him warily. "And then?"

He took a deep breath and extended his olive branch. "I promise to try to lighten up around you if you agree to keep working for my family."

She arched one eyebrow. "And I can come and go as I please? I won't have to stay at your cabin and wear clothes that don't belong to me?"

He sighed, but nodded. He knew that was coming, and he wasn't ready to let her go. They had too many unresolved feelings, and she was still learning how to adjust to her new way of life. But if he tried to force her hand, he'd push her away. "But if you decide to just leave and never return, I want you to talk to me. No one else. Got it?"

She smiled at him and nodded. "Got it."

Well, that was a start.

CHAPTER SEVEN

Lilly stepped out of the shower at her house after another long day of work with renewed motivation. Three days ago, Jack had come running to her when he'd realized she'd left, and she'd actually gotten him to compromise on their situation without any trouble. But next time she should be careful with what she was asking for. She hadn't realized that not staying with him had meant no sex for her!

At first she'd been relieved he wasn't tempting her because sex would just confuse her more. She was all over the place emotionally when it came to that hottie with the body. There were moments when she wanted to strangle him, as in wrap-her-fingers-around-his-thickly-muscled-neck-

and-squeeze-the-life-out-of-him-until-he-quit-breathing kill-him moments. And then there were times when she felt like squealing as if she were a love-struck teenager when she saw him. Sweaty palms? Check. Butterflies in the tummy? Check. Yeah, that just made her want to puke a little in her mouth.

But the no sex thing? That had to come to an end.

Okay, so she was being a little selfish. Jack did have other issues to deal with. He'd tried talking to his family the last two nights at dinner about what he'd discovered regarding his mother, but the first night, Mikaela wasn't feeling well, so she and Josh had stayed home. Hadn't that been just peachy?

Without Mikaela there, that left only Krista and Ariel as the other women. One sister had been attacked by the man she... by Jack—she still didn't know how to refer to him—and the other was protective of that sister, so conversations had been strained where Lillian was concerned. And then last night, Rob and Ariel had been MIA. At least Krista had been friendlier last night. And with the news quickly spreading this morning as to why Ariel and Rob hadn't been at dinner, Lillian understood why Krista had been chipper. Ariel and Rob had mated. Apparently that was a long time coming. But because of that mating, Lillian was doubtful Jack would have an opportunity to discuss the news of his family tonight since everyone would be celebrating the lovebirds' *choice* to mate.

Jack still wanted her there, though, and like the dutiful little kitten, she'd followed. But this time, she was going to get something in return since she figured there was no way in hell Jack would bring up the family topic tonight and rain on the newly mated lovebirds' parade. No, the evening would be short, and she could get herself invited back to Jack's place for some lovin'.

That was the plan anyway.

She put on some jeans, sexy boots, and a light cashmere sweater. The baby blue color really complemented her eyes. She grabbed her jacket, locked up the house, and headed toward her four-wheeler.

The ride there had been quick, the night air too cool already. Thankfully, she'd talked Jack into leaving the gate open between the old property lines, so she wouldn't have to stop and use the keys she'd swiped when she'd left the other day. All this locking and unlocking business was just silly anyway.

She started to park close to the house, but decided it'd be best to park close to Jack's cabin instead. At least then if he tried to let her down gently, she'd have a reason to go to his cabin afterward.

Then I'll just seduce him.

She chuckled as she parked her ride on the side of the cabin and walked toward the main house. Her little kitty cat was giving up the goods tonight come hell or high water.

When she pushed open the door to the dining room, her eyes immediately sought out Jack. And may she be stricken down if he wasn't gorgeous, tanned with piercing blue eyes. The others all had green or green-blue mixed, but Jack's were startling blue. Sexy.

And those eyes were fixed on her.

She smirked when she headed toward him, only to hesitate when she got close. Thomas was standing by, and he turned toward her.

"It's lovely to see you this evening, Lillian. We have much to celebrate tonight."

She smiled and nodded, and then looked at Ariel and Rob standing arm in arm. "I heard. Congratulations." Funny thing was, she'd meant it. Maybe she and Jack's mating had been accidental—and when had she stopped blaming only him?—but Rob and Ariel had entered into theirs on their own terms. She was truly happy for them.

Ariel stepped over to her and hugged her. Lillian startled, but put her arms around Ariel and returned the gesture.

"Thank you," Ariel whispered. Then she pulled back and looked at Lillian with a wicked smile.

"Don't be surprised if we cut out of here early tonight. I've doused myself with catnip."

A surprised laugh escaped Lillian's lips before she pressed them together.

"What are you talking about over there?" Rob asked as he stepped over. He was glowing, and when Ariel smiled at him, Lillian felt a little twinge of regret. Why couldn't her mating have been as loving as theirs must have been?

She automatically looked up, shocked that she'd even thought that, and immediately saw Jack watching her with confusion. Crap. She smiled at him, trying to forget the craziness that had just whispered through her mind. It was done. There was no going back. Besides, she didn't want him to worry about what she was thinking. She wanted him horny. She didn't have time for regrets of any nature.

She quickly pointed to the bar and then mimicked sipping from a glass, indicating she wanted him to get her a drink as both a distraction for him and a balm for her sudden jitters.

Jack nodded and stepped over to the bar to pour her a drink, when Jeffery walked in.

"Ah, time for dinner," Thomas said. "We can continue prying into Rob and Ariel's business while we eat." He chuckled as they all made their way to the table.

"'Bout time you made an honest woman outta her," Toby said as he lightly punched Rob in the arm.

"Honest woman? I don't see a ring on your mate's finger, Toby," Josh said.

Toby blushed and quickly looked at Krista. She just giggled and shook her head as she took her seat.

"Um, we're not talking about us. We're talking about Rob and Ariel," Toby said lamely as he sat down.

Lilly stood at her chair just taking in the good-natured ribbing. She hadn't had a family like this, and it felt nice to see everyone enjoying each other's company.

Jack came over to Lillian's seat and placed her beverage on the table as he slid his hand onto her back. His lips brushed her ear. "You look beautiful, Lilly."

"Thanks," she breathed. And if she were being brutally honest, she did like the way he called her Lilly. It felt private, as though he was meant to be the only one to ever call her that.

He pulled the chair out for her and helped her get seated before walking to the other side of the table and to his own chair.

As Lillian had expected, the conversation was focused solely on Rob and Ariel. They both seemed lighter than air, but no way was she going to think about her feelings on their mating. She didn't need any more envious thoughts sneaking up on her. Instead, she ate and watched Jack. Every now and then, their eyes would lock, and she'd smile behind her glass. Once she even got a wink out of him. God, and if that wasn't like lighting a flame under those butterflies in her belly, she didn't know what was.

After everyone finished eating, the conversation shifted to more mundane topics, and people started to stand. It was time to make her move. She stood and stretched, making sure her insanely large boobs were thrust forward. When she relaxed her arms, she looked nonchalantly around the room.

Great. Jack's back was to her. She sighed and picked up her drink. She'd have to be more direct.

Lillian walked over to Jack and rubbed his arm as she circled to face him.

"I'm glad you're here," he murmured. Then he looked to the side. "Before everybody leaves, I think we should talk about something I've found."

Oh crap! He was holding that dang photo. So he was going to broach the topic tonight. There went her night of sexing. She downed her drink and stood beside him for what was sure to be an interesting night for reasons she hadn't been planning on.

"What's that?" Rob asked, stepping forward.

"A photo I found of Mom and some other people when I was in Dad's office," Jack said as he watched Thomas.

The color drained from Thomas's face. Apparently he didn't need any further clarification to understand what photo Jack was holding.

"Relax, Dad. It's okay," Josh said as he leveled his shoulders and looked at Jack.

"Holy shit! You knew?" Well, well, well, apparently Josh didn't need any more clarification either.

"Yes," Josh said evenly. He glanced at Mikaela, who was rubbing her tummy a little too quickly to actually be soothing.

"What the hell is going on?" Toby asked as he walked closer to Jack.

Jack handed him the photo. "Read the back," he gritted out.

Thomas seemed to finally get his wits about him to some degree because he shuffled over, but his mind was obviously somewhere else.

Rob peered around Toby to read along with him.

"I guess it's time you all knew."

"You're damn right," Jack blurted out. Lillian rubbed his arm. She didn't want him doing or saying anything he'd regret later. To her relief, he leaned into her slightly.

"What the fuck is this, Dad? And why are we just finding this out?" Rob snapped while he glared at Josh.

"I just found out a few months ago. After Mikaela got pregnant. It's not like I've known all along."

"But you didn't say anything? Hell, *that* was the reason I wanted to talk to you a couple of weeks ago!" he yelled as he pointed to the incriminating picture.

"Settle down!" Thomas roared.

Lillian jumped at the authoritative tone she'd never heard come out of the patriarch before. Jack wrapped his arm around her, but he didn't look at her. It seemed as if it was a subconscious gesture, one she was more than willing to take.

"Joshua didn't say anything to any-body because this is my story to tell. The only reason I told him is because his mate is pregnant, and it could become an issue."

"Would you like for us to leave, Thomas, so you can talk to your sons in private?" Ariel motioned toward the women in the room as she asked.

"No, that will not be necessary. You are all my sons' mates. This involves you, too." He sighed as he leaned against the wall. "This story is long overdue, and I want to make sure you all understand because this is not going to be a topic open for discussion again."

Lillian slipped out of Jack's arms to pour herself and Jack another drink. The other women picked up on the hint and got drinks for their men and themselves, except Mikaela, who got juice. Mikaela obviously knew what was going on, but the two sisters looked a little shell-shocked.

"I met Felina Lyons on a fall day not unlike today." Thomas wasn't looking at anyone. His eyes were glazed as if he'd retreated to that place he'd visited as soon as the topic of the photo began. "She was a vision." He sighed and looked at Jack. "And off-limits."

"Because she was some sort of queen?"

Thomas half smiled. "Not yet, but she was destined to be. You see, we were raised with several prides of mountain lion shifters. There was a caste system similar to that of historical European classes. Your mother was of the royalty class and was betrothed to a male from an elite pride. I was raised within a working-class pride, which consisted of people who were not of the purest blood."

"So there are others like us?" Rob asked.

"Oh yes. And shifters of other animals as well. But we all have our own vices. The mountain lion shifters will mate with any available female. Bear shifters are much more aggressive when it comes to women, but they can be around unmated females. Wolf shifters are extremely territorial but loyal."

He shifted and rubbed his head. "The day I met your mother was the day I felt alive. She was with an army of protectors, all mated, of course. And when I looked into her eyes, I just knew she was meant for me.

"I was working the field, and she came up to me. She introduced herself and asked if she could contact me. I couldn't tell her no. Not because she was the future queen of our people but because in that moment, I knew I'd do whatever she'd ask of me for the rest of my life.

"We began an affair of the heart. We exchanged letters with the help of some family members and staff. She got me a job on the royalty's official estate so we could see each other—not alone, never alone. But across the courtyard, by the pond, near the stables, wherever we could arrange accidental meetings."

Lillian watched Jack as Thomas continued, the anger fleeing with each word his father spoke.

"The first time I ever touched your mother was the night we mated. We arranged it ourselves because it was what we both wanted. She picked me, and I will love her for all eternity."

When Thomas didn't continue, Jack asked, "So why not just tell us?"

Something dark flashed across Thomas's face. "Because when her betrothed discovered what had happened, he tried to kill me. I, a man so beneath him, had succeeded in taking away something he felt belonged to him. But I was on my way to see your mother, and the vile man ended up killing my family instead. Your mother and I fled that night. She decided we'd live a life in solitude, away from the bureaucracy of her destiny, forge our own journey in life. She notified her family of her intentions, and then they really started hating me. Blamed me for brainwashing her, kidnapping her, whatever they could think of. But over the years, they finally learned to accept our decision. They never knew we gave birth to children until years after you were all born. They don't even know where we live."

"Then how was she able to maintain contact with your family?" Krista asked.

"That was my doing," Jeffery said, and everyone turned to look at him. Lillian could see she wasn't the only one gaping at him.

Thomas smiled. "Ah, yes. Jeffery is more than just a helping hand around here."

Jeffery walked up and stood next to Thomas. "If I may?"

Thomas nodded at him.

"I was one of the people who delivered

the letters between our fair Felina and Thomas and helped organize their accidental meetings and eventual joining. When they fled, I came with them and have facilitated communications ever since."

"So you're a mountain lion shifter, too?"

"Not exactly," Jeffery said, a small smile playing at the corner of his lips. "I'm—how did you phrase it, Thomas?—extremely territorial but loyal."

Lillian gasped, but the sound was echoed throughout the room.

"You're a werewolf?" Mikaela shrieked. Okay, so maybe she and Josh didn't know everything. Josh also had that stricken look his brothers were all sporting.

"Werewolves are myths. He's a shifter," Thomas said. "Jeffery comes from a pack of wolf shifters who have been guarding the royal bloodline for centuries."

"So let me get this straight," Jack said as he pinched the bridge of his nose and briefly squeezed his eyes shut. "Mom was supposed to be a queen, but she defied her obligation to mate with a specific man and chose you instead. You two mated. Her intended retaliated, and innocent people suffered. Then you fled for safety and serenity. Did I forget anything?"

"No, but now we come to the reason I had to discuss this with Josh a few months ago," Thomas said. "The Lyons pride is a matriarchal society. Part of the reason your instinct is to wait for your mate to eat and always watch out for her is because you know inside that you must defer to her. You are the stronger one, the protector, but she is the leader.

"Your mother was destined to be the queen, the first queen in many years because several generations before her had given birth to sons. Having a female baby in the Lyons bloodline is something to rejoice and is very sacred. If no female is born, then the eldest son will reign in her place, but he will always and willfully defer to a female of Lyons blood." Thomas sighed. "You see, if Mikaela and Josh give birth to a female, then it could change things. They should have the right to return to the royal estate. Not only is Josh Lina's eldest son, which means he can rightfully take leadership now, but if he has a daughter, then he had a right to know what could come of that if he chooses to return to that life."

"We all run the risk of having a daughter," Toby said. "You should have shared this with us, too, Dad."

"Probably so. Joshua has been encouraging me to do just that, so don't blame him for not saying anything. But after what we'd discussed, I decided it was best to wait until Mikaela gave birth."

"And what was discussed?" Rob asked, arms crossed.

"That I'm not going anywhere," Josh snapped. "It doesn't matter to me where we come from. It matters where we are now. Mom chose this life for us, and I intend to respect that decision and honor her wish."

Mikaela leaned into her husband and said, "We agreed we'd revisit the matter if we gave birth to a daughter, but since the chances of that are very slim, there was no need to stress about it. As far as we're concerned, this is our life." Then she looked up at her husband. "My feet are aching. Can we take this conversation into the den so we can sit down and get comfortable?"

Josh kissed the top of her head. "Of course."

Lillian followed alongside Jack to the den, where drinks were refilled and everyone got comfortable on the couch. The night was long and filled with stories that she'd never thought she'd ever hear in her life. If there weren't times that Jack looked like a little lost boy trying to take in all this new information, she might have actually freaked out. But to her, everything was new anyway. She just sat down beside him and held his hand while the conversation continued, while the life he'd always known changed into something totally different. Being his rock.

His mate.

And knowing there was no other place she'd rather be than right here beside him.

CHAPTER EIGHT

JACK WALKED BACK to his cabin with Lilly next to him. He'd been holding her hand and couldn't seem to let go, so he'd been relieved when she said she'd parked next to his cabin—he could hold on to her a little longer, draw from her strength.

His mind was swimming with all he'd just learned. Everything was so much more complicated than he'd originally thought, but now that he knew the truth, it was hard to stay angry at his father for not telling them all along about their true heritage. He could dwell on what his parents should have said a long time ago, but the truth was it was done. They'd made the decision not to say anything to them until a need to do so had come up, and they'd stuck to that decision. He might not have agreed with it completely, but he respected it.

When Lilly walked to the door of his cabin and not to the side where she'd parked her four-wheeler, he hesitated, his thoughts shifting to the present. God, he didn't want her to leave. He hated her not being there the last couple of nights. But he didn't want her to think he was just after her body. He forced himself to let go of her hand.

"I can see myself in," he mumbled. "Good night." He leaned down to kiss her cheek, but she turned her head at the last second, and their lips grazed.

Her tongue prodded his lips, seeking entry, and he opened on a groan. Oh, how he'd missed the taste of her. That devilish tongue rubbed across his, and he had to lock his knees to keep from crumpling. If only she knew how much he needed this. Needed her. He clutched her waist, and her cool fingers slid around his neck and into his hair as she deepened the kiss. He returned it with fervor, drinking from her as if he'd never get to do it again.

When she pulled back, he dropped his forehead to hers and tried pulling air into his burning lungs, his erection straining against his jeans. He couldn't force her to come inside. He wouldn't. He just had to find the strength to let go of her and think of that kiss as her way of saying good night to him.

"You know, I'd planned on seducing you tonight because I wanted you to fuck me."

He moaned at her words and shifted, trying not to rub his cock against her. She wasn't making this easy for him at all.

"Now I know you need it, too."

"I need *you*, not it," he rasped. He wanted her to understand that.

"That's very noble of you, big guy." She straightened and took his hand. "Follow me."

She turned, opened the door, and pulled him inside.

And he let her.

They didn't say anything while she guided him to the bed. The lights were left off, but the glow of the moon illuminated the room enough that he could see her.

Lilly reached up and unbuttoned his shirt, and Jack just stood motionless, rapt in her beauty. Once she'd gotten his shirt off, she kneeled before him and unfastened his jeans, the rasp of the zipper a sigh of relief as his erection sprang free. She pushed his pants and underwear down to his knees and grabbed his ass. Oh shit! She leaned forward and licked along the ridge of his cock and sucked the head into her mouth.

He couldn't hold still any longer. Jack fisted his fingers in her hair and widened his stance as much as he could within the confines of his jeans to help balance himself. He'd tasted her, feasted on her pussy several times, but he hadn't allowed her to do this for him yet. It was too easy for him to lose the control he barely kept a hold of when she was around him like this. But he wanted her. He wanted anything she wanted to give him, and so he'd hold her and let her take whatever she wanted from him.

"So good," he moaned as his head fell back. Her tongue was torturing the sensitive notch before taking him deeper.

She hummed as her head started bobbing faster, and he gritted his teeth to hold back his need to come when she reached up and caressed his balls. With her other hand, she stroked his cock while she sucked him, and his hands clenched in her hair, wanting to force her to take all of him. He held himself back, though, not wanting to take control of what she was doing.

But then she did it anyway. By God, she took him to the back of her throat and swallowed, milking him. He was going to blow.

But he wasn't ready to be finished. Not yet.

Jack pulled her off him, unable to help the preejaculate from steadily leaking from the tip, and the little minx lapped it while he tried to get her to her feet.

He grabbed the hem of her sweater and yanked it off her body. She fumbled with her jeans while he got his the rest of the way off, and within moments, they were both completely naked.

"Come here," he breathed as he stepped up to her. He pulled her into his arms and kissed her, nipped at her lips, suckled her tongue, licked her lips. He couldn't get enough, but he was trying to take his time about it. He gently eased her onto the bed while he continued to pull drugging kisses from her. Once she was completely beneath him, he shifted, kissing a path to her neck, her shoulder, her collar-bone. He'd used one arm to prop himself up, freeing one hand to explore. He glided it along her waist, to her breast. He gently raked his fingers over the budding nipple of one while his mouth found the other.

Lillian arched her back and moaned, her pleasure heightening his. He sucked her nipple into his mouth as he pinched the other one. She writhed beneath him, rubbing herself against his aching cock, but he couldn't let go of her long enough to sate his need. Her need was his. Her desire was all his body and soul cared about.

He moved his mouth to her other breast and gave it the same treatment as the first one, kissing it, loving it until it was ruddy and taut. He alternated between the two, peppering kisses between them when he traveled back and forth, and as he continued his ministrations, the smell of her arousal grew with each draw from his lips, lick of his tongue, each passing second.

When he finally released her, he forged a path to the apex of her thighs, kissing and nibbling on all the places his lips landed, his hands stroking, roaming over her wherever he could reach. She was soft, smooth, decadent, a taste that was uniquely all Lilly, a flavor as spicy as her attitude, as savory as her heart.

"Please," she breathed, and only then did he realize he'd neglected her clit in his path of rediscovery.

"Say it again," he whispered.

And she did, repeatedly, until he licked from her opening to her clit. As soon as his tongue touched her there, she grabbed his head, pushing him onto her even further. So he gave her what she wanted.

He circled her clit a few times and then drew it into his mouth and sucked. Her legs stiffened and her hips began to pump, seeking her orgasm. God, she was so wet. Jack wanted to feel her coming, so he pushed two fingers into her and rubbed that sweet spot within. He felt the beginning spasms just before she screamed his name in ecstasy. And he still didn't want to stop. He kept sucking and batting her clit with his tongue and fucking her with his fingers. He was so hard, he was grinding himself against her leg, seeking a little relief, but unable to stop tasting her enough to fuck her in earnest.

Lilly screamed again and bucked

against him, so he fingered her harder and tongued her clit with lightning-fast strokes. She was trembling and sobbing when she came down, and he couldn't wait any longer. Jack climbed up onto of her, angled her limp legs around his hips, and slowly eased his cock into her.

So hot. A scorching vise. He knew he wouldn't be able to last long, so he had to go slowly. He pushed all the way in and waited for her pulsing pussy to adjust to him.

He kissed the hollow behind her ear. "You feel like heaven."

"Don't stop."

He moaned, pulled out slowly, and then pushed into her a little harder. She moaned, and he did it again, increasing his pace with each thrust. He was mindless with need, a need so powerful he didn't know how to describe it. It was an ache so deep that he knew no one else would ever to be able to fill it.

Only his Lilly. Forever.

He fucked her harder, and she met his thrusts with her own while mumbling unintelligible words. He felt his heart exploding and slammed his mouth down onto hers before any words spilled out that he wasn't ready to express.

She wailed into his mouth as her pussy contracted violently around him, pushing him over the edge. He kept pumping into her until he was spent, sweaty, exhausted. And he still continued to kiss her, too greedy to let go of her mouth.

Too scared he'd tell her how much he was in love with her if he did.

LILLIAN WAS in love with him. She wasn't sure when it had happened, but somewhere along the way, it had. Last night had started as an evening to get her groove on, then downshifted into one of serious family business where she went from temptress to supporter. But in the end, she'd succeeded in getting Jack in bed. But it had been more. So much more. They hadn't just had sex.

They'd made love. The kind of joining she'd only dreamed about but never thought she'd ever get to experience in her life.

After the first time, they'd done it twice

more. Jack had left no part of her body unexplored. He'd been tender, caring, passionate. He'd been so attentive to her that it was as if she were some goddess he worshipped. He'd made her feel beautiful. He'd made her feel loved.

After several hours of emotionally raw sex, they'd woken up to another round of burning need that had to be satisfied. She was physically and spiritually exhausted, but she also knew she wasn't ready to let him go just because her night with him was over. They hadn't really discussed living arrangements, but the need to see where things were going between them drove her to go home this morning and pack a bag.

A small bag. Just a few changes of clothing, her toothbrush, some necessities. She wasn't going to just move in. She was still getting to know him. Besides, the thought of making that leap right now was just a little terrifying, even though she knew how she felt about him. But she could do this with baby steps, plan for a few nights at a time, maybe work her way up to a week. Yeah, that sounded much easier for her to accept.

She was on her four-wheeler heading to

her house when she came up to the gate and stopped.

Locked again. She sighed as she got off her ride and walked to it. She was going to have to talk to Jack about this damn gate. It was silly to stop every time and unlock it. When she pulled on the padlock to position the key she'd commandeered, it slipped opened. Odd, so it hadn't been locked, just hanging. She pulled the padlock off, lifted the bar, and pushed the gate open. After she got on her wheeler and drove through, she pushed the gate to and locked it.

She drove the rest of the way to her father's house thinking about Jack and the strange path her life had taken. Strange, but right. Deep down it felt as if he was what was always meant for her. Lillian had never believed in fate like this, but believing and experiencing were two different things.

I'm in love with a man who turns into a cat and was born to a queen of the cat people. She giggled. She couldn't make this shit up.

She rounded the last bend to her father's house and frowned as she neared it. The light in the kitchen was on, and she knew she'd turned out all the lights. Her father was anal about wasting electricity. *Dad.* She drove around to where her father usually parked and saw his truck was there. So he was finally home. She killed the engine to her wheeler and went in through the back door.

Lillian froze.

Her father was sitting at the kitchen table wearing hunter's fatigues and face paint. His eyes were red, as if he hadn't slept in five days, and there was a rank odor coming from him that hinted he probably hadn't showered in as many either.

"Dad?" she muttered, stepping closer on shaky legs. What the hell was he doing? "When did you get back from Grandma's?"

He huffed as he lifted a coffee cup and took a sip. "Didn't go see her."

The hair on the back of her neck stood. Why was he just staring at her? "Why not? What's going on?"

"You just had to go and ruin my plan." He slammed his cup down, and she jumped, too shocked to understand anything.

"I-I don't know what you mean."

He snarled at her, the disdain in his expression filling her with foreboding. "I wanted you to work for them, not fuck one of them."

"You're not making any sense, Dad." What did he mean he wanted her to work for them? He hated the Woods family. And how did he know she'd been sleeping with Jack?

He rose slowly and placed his palm flat on the table to help balance himself. She looked down and saw dried blood around ripped camouflaged pants. He was hurt, but whatever had injured him, he wasn't letting it stop him completely. He had a look of fierce determination in his eyes. And frankly, it was scaring the hell out of her.

"Does the name Rodrick Lyons ring a bell?"

Hmm... she wasn't sure about the Rodrick part, but the name Lyons had her heart pounding. That was Jack's mother's maiden name. That word had been said a lot last night. Not that she knew where her dad was going with this. She shook her head quickly, but couldn't voice her response to him.

"I knew those people over there were

off," he said, righteous indignation heavy in his voice.

"Always in our business. Stole my company when the recession hit. Should've known they were just a bunch of mutants."

Oh God. He knew. He knew their secret. She just stood there, watching him, not sure what to say.

Part of her wanted to defend the family who'd been nothing but nice to her, but another part of her knew if she tried that her father might go ballistic.

"I don't understand what you're talking about, Dad," she said slowly, trying to make him focus. If she knew what was going on, then she would be better prepared deal with him.

"Stupid girl. You were never that smart." He sighed. "A representative of Mr. Lyons contacted me. Asked me to investigate my neighbors. Told me some crazy story about them turning into large cats and that I'd have to cover my scent and scout at night to see them. He gave me ten grand to start and offered me fifty if I got proof. I tried to get the evidence on my own, but didn't have any luck, so I set you up to work for them. I figured if I got you access to their property, I'd get what I needed."

"So that's why you didn't get mad when I told you I was going to work there."

He laughed sarcastically. "Hell, Lillian, I told you *you* should go show them dick-heads how to do the job right."

Shit. "So you used me."

He shrugged. "I just nudged you in the right direction." Then he frowned. "I didn't mean for you to go fuck one of them. Did he bite you? That man said they can turn people into lions if they bite them. Are you one of those freaks now, too?"

Lillian swallowed and tried to carefully construct her response. She needed to find a way to get out of here and warn Jack what was going on, but she wouldn't be able to do that if her father knew the truth. The man was crazy.

"No, he didn't bite me. Are you going to tell me how you know I slept with him?"

His father's fist slammed onto the table. "I saw him kissing you outside one of those cabins last night while doing surveillance and watched you walk inside with him. Have you no shame?" he roared.

At least he hadn't watched her run

around as a mountain lion and fuck Jack in the woods. That would've been a little harder to lie about. "Dad, whoever that Mr. Lyons person is, they have to be lying to you. There's no such thing as people who turn into animals."

"That's what I thought, too. But I've seen those cats running around at night. Just haven't been able to see them turning into the creatures." Her dad started pacing.

"Because they don't exist. Dad, this is —" A low moan came from the other room, cutting her off.

"What the hell was that?"

He stopped and smiled. "Something better than pictures. I caught me one of them. Put up a nasty little fight, too."

Shit, shit, shit. Which one had he managed to overtake? No wonder he was injured, and the sound from the other room sounded like a painful one. *God, please don't let it be Jack.* She needed to find out who was in the living room and figure a way out of here before her dad did something really crazy, like skin whoever was in there and sell the hide.

"You can't be serious. You can't just kidnap someone," she screeched.

He laughed maniacally, and whatever blood was in her face drained in an instant. Her father's cheese had totally slipped off his cracker.

"Oh, I didn't. *You* did. Why do you think the gate has been unlocked so many times? I snuck into the house on your first day and got a key made to the gate between our properties. I decided I needed a fall guy, and you're it, sweetheart. I've tampered with the gate, and if that wasn't enough, I left a ransom note to clear up any suspicions. Signed by you."

"What is wrong with you?" she yelled and ran for the living room. Lillian didn't have time to devise a great escape plan. She'd just have to garner some willpower to help her with the man her father had been able to drag back here.

She skidded to a halt when she saw a pair of green eyes glazed over, staring at her, and who they belonged to. The body was bloody and limp. She'd have fallen to her knees and sobbed if her legs worked. "No," she breathed. *Please, God, no.*

"Yes, Lillian. This is much better, don't you think? Mr. Lyons wanted proof that these people could shift into animals, and not only did I manage to trap me one, but just image how much money he'll give me now that I got me one who is carrying one of the spawns."

"Mikaela."

CHAPTER NINE

SOMETHING WAS WRONG. Lilly hadn't returned after her midday disappearing act, and the last time she'd done this, she'd run from him. Back home. Jack had tried radioing her, but she wouldn't answer. She was either ignoring him or she was out of range, which meant she had left. Both options just pissed him off. Why would she just run away from him after what they'd shared last night?

There was something wrong, all right—Jack was a fool.

He'd thought after the night they'd shared that Lilly would actually open up to him a little more, maybe try to consider sharing a life with him. He didn't expect her to marry him tomorrow and just live happily ever after, but he sure as hell hadn't expected her to just cut and run either. He wanted to storm after her, drag her back here, and tie her to his bed until she accepted him as her mate. But he wouldn't keep running after her. At some point, she'd have to come to him. He knew that the possibility of that happening was very slim, and his heart ached at the thought of his mate not being around, but he had his pride.

A roar pierced his ears, and he stiffened. "Josh," he mumbled. At the same time, static flared on his radio.

"Jack, come in," Rob said.

He lifted the handheld device up to his mouth. "Yeah?"

"We need you in the office. Now, man. Hurry."

He didn't sign off. He hopped on his wheeler and sped to the main house. He threw it in park and bolted up the stairs and into the house. The scents of his family were the strongest in the office area, so he quickly made his way there. When he pushed open the door, the smell of blood assaulted him and his nose wrinkled as he scanned the room. Josh was breathing hard, a look that could be described only as a combination of overwhelming grief and uncontrollable rage marring his expression.

"What's going on?"

Josh's head snapped in Jack's direction, and he took a threatening step toward him. Rob and Toby grabbed him and held him back.

"What the fuck?"

"Where. Is. My. Wife?" Josh growled, vehemence dripping from his words.

Jack's hands went up in placation. "I don't know, bro. What's wrong?"

"Come here," Thomas said. He and Jeffery were standing next to the desk in the room.

Jack went, but didn't understand why everyone was staring at him as though he'd eaten baby kittens for lunch.

"Where is Lillian?" Thomas asked.

Jack stopped, his stomach dropping. "I don't know. She didn't return after her midmorning break."

"Look at this, but don't touch it. We called a forensics team."

Jack felt the blood rushing through his veins when he stepped closer. His head was swimming for the second time within twenty-four hours, but instead of like last night, when he got some closure to long-unanswered questions, this feeling made him sick. Until he started to read a note that was covered in blood. Then he wanted to vomit.

Crazy cat people,

My job here is done, and the pregnant one is coming with me. My buyer will surely pay top dollar for her.

Lillian

No, no, no, no, no, no, no, no. No way. No. Fucking. Way. "No!"

"You need to tell us everything you've talked about, Jackson."

The world was tilting. He grabbed his head and roared as he hunched over. She wouldn't do this to him. To his family.

Would she?

She didn't want to be with him. She'd insulted him at every opportunity.

"We found a padlock by the letter, too," Jeffery said. "It's the same style as the one used at the gate closest to their property."

"Did you give her a key to that gate, Jackson?" Thomas asked sternly.

Hell no, he hadn't. But he'd known she'd taken one because that was the way she'd come and go.

He shook his head.

Josh wailed. "I need to find Mikaela right now!" He forcefully shrugged their brothers off him and leveled a stare at Jack. "You're going to help me."

"We have to wait for the forensics. I'm sure the Lyons are sending a task force with top-notch investigators," Thomas said and then looked away. "And doctors."

Josh moaned, agony pouring out of him. "With every second, that *woman* is getting farther away from here with my wife. My *baby*. My life!"

"I said she was a bitch," Toby barked. "She forced her way into a job. Then she gets you drunk and gets you to mate with her, and now she's taken Mikaela. She'd been fucking playing us all along."

"She used you, son," Thomas said, placing a hand on his shoulder. "Jeffery tried calling in some reinforcements, but for as many people as we need here, they had to confront the Lyons for approval.

They know everything now. But it doesn't matter. We must do whatever it takes to find Mikaela before Lillian hurts her, too."

Hurt? No, Jack wasn't being hurt. He was being killed. He couldn't breathe. The gaping hole in his chest was making it difficult for him to even move. He couldn't even see. Everything was blurry.

Then he felt wetness touch his cheek, and he roared as the emotion spilled over. If Lillian was so evil, there was only one thing that could be done. She knew too much, and she was out to harm his family. She couldn't be allowed to get away with it.

And live.

He looked at Josh. If they stood a chance of finding them, they couldn't wait for help. "Let's go."

———

THEY WERE deep in the woods. Lillian's insane father had doused the house and his car with gasoline and lit everything. He'd made her carry Mikaela, whom he'd drugged, because he was too weak from his battle with her. At first Lillian had refused to carry her, but then he started pouring the gas all over the place and said he didn't care, that Mikaela could just burn and he could go grab one of the others to sell. She'd had no other choice but to carry her friend out of there because she wouldn't let anything else happen to Mikaela if she could help it.

Thankfully, her father hadn't suspected Lillian was lying about being bitten. He was a large man, so if she stood a fighting chance with him, she'd have to shift and attack him in her feral form. But she'd have to wait until they got to a point where she could put Mikaela safely out of harm's way.

She didn't need her father killing Mikaela and running off.

They'd been hiking for hours, though, and they could still see the smoke in the distance. If that fire wasn't contained, thousands of acres and years of work would be ruined. But more important to their immediate situation, they could be trapped in a burning forest.

It was now or never. Lillian had to do something before her father guided them even farther into the woods. She saw a rock embedded in the path and tripped. She went down on one knee and screamed, all the while carefully keeping Mikaela from sliding off her shoulder and falling.

Her dad grunted and turned around. Lillian struggled to stand and hopped on her foot. "I need a break."

"Damn it, girl. We don't have time for this."

"Five minutes." She shuffled over to the edge of the path, making sure her limps were exaggerated, and gently released Mikaela, propping her up against a tree. When she stood, she tried stretching, but made sure she didn't favor her "sprained" ankle.

Lillian hobbled back toward her dad, but continued past him a ways, scouting the path, hoping it looked as though she was eager to get away with her father and not away from him. "So how much farther do we have?" she asked as she wiped the sweat from her brow and faced him.

"About three more miles."

Shit. That'd take at least two hours with her carrying Mikaela. Lillian wasn't sure if it'd be faster to go back the way they came once she got them away from her father or to continue on the path.

Then again, maybe there was

someone waiting for them at the end of the trail. She couldn't take that chance. She glanced at the orange glow of the forest below and knew she had only one choice.

They'd have to go back.

Which meant she really didn't have any more time to waste.

"I need to pee," she mumbled and headed toward the edge of the trail to seek out cover to take off her clothes.

"Hurry up. We gotta get a move on."

"Okay."

Once she was out of sight, she quickly shucked her clothes and shifted, amazed at how natural it felt for her to be like this now. It was a part of her, a part she hadn't even known she was missing until she'd found it—found Jack. God, and he thought she'd betrayed him. Would he forgive her once he knew the truth, or would he still hate her for what her father had done to Mikaela? She hoped Mikaela woke up soon. She'd been out for about three hours now, and Lillian was worried what that'd mean for the baby.

Lillian sunk as close to the ground as she could and crawled to the edge of the forest. Her father was at the edge of the trail opposite her, taking a leak.

She closed her eyes for a brief moment, knowing that she'd have to stop her father with any means necessary. It was him or them, a decision that was made the moment he'd kidnapped Mikaela and taken them both hostage.

She charged, but a sound to her right just before she hit her father caught her by surprise. She looked just in time to see another lion reach him first and feel another one knock her to the ground, stealing her breath.

"I'm going to kill you," Jack raged as he rolled with her. She heard the other lion screaming in his head and knew it was Josh, but the growls he was making as he ripped her father's throat out drowned out the oaths he was swearing.

"Stop! You have to help Mikaela!" Lillian struggled with Jack, but he was far too strong for her.

"That's what we're here to do. I can't believe you'd actually betray me like this. And to think I actually thought I fucking loved you. Shit!"

His admission distracted her enough

that she lost her footing and tumbled over again.

"It's not what you think, Jack. Please."

"Mikaela!" Josh screamed as he ran around in his human form, naked.

Lillian shifted, her hands now fisting in Jack's fur as she tried pushing him off her. "She's beside the oak tree on the south side."

Jack shifted and grabbed her hands to hold them above her head. "You think you'll have a fighting chance like this instead?" he asked, incredulous.

"She's over here! Help me!" Josh sounded frantic.

Jack hesitated getting off her to help his brother. His eyes narrowed, and his grip tightened. "Fuck!"

Jack jumped up and ran toward Josh. Lillian scrambled to her feet and shuffled over there.

"You stay the fuck back!" Jack roared at her as he helped Josh lift Mikaela.

"She's bleeding everywhere. Oh God, what did you do to her?" Josh bellowed.

"I-I didn't do anything. My father took her and drugged her. I don't know what he gave her. Just please help her."

Josh hoisted Mikaela up into his arms. "Kitten? I'm here, baby. I'm here." Then he looked at Jack.

"We're going to run through the trees to get to the house faster. I need you in front to forge a path for us since I won't be able to block limbs while I carry her."

Jack nodded. "On it." He started to turn, but stopped and looked at Lillian. His hands were fisted, and his arms were shaking. His eyes the hardest, coldest she'd ever seen. He was lethal, and in that moment, she'd never feared him more. "You are dead to me, Lillian. If I ever see you again, I'll make you dead to everyone else. You so much as breathe a word about my family to anyone, I'll hunt you down like the rabid little animal you are and kill you slowly. And after that, I will *bathe in your blood!*" He yelled the last words, the force of them ruffling her hair as he screamed at her.

Then he turned and ran with Josh right on his heels.

Mikaela had been rescued. It was what she'd wanted, but as she slumped to the ground, naked and crying next to her father's dead body, all she could think was she'd lost the only family she'd loved in a very long time.

Because she knew from the look on Jack's face and the force of his words that he'd never let her explain or ever forgive her if he learned the truth from somewhere else.

She was all alone now.

JACK PACED OUTSIDE of the room where four doctors were working on Mikaela. Josh was a wreck, and their father and brothers were teaming around him to try to comfort him. He could tell Josh was barely hanging on to sanity while his wife and child fought for their lives. The only time he'd seen Josh cry was when their mother had died, but that was different. His older brother looked as if he was ready to welcome death if the doctors didn't come out of the room with good news.

Jack's own destroyed heart paled in comparison. He didn't deserve to feel agony after what Lillian had done to him. How could he? If he'd thought with his head and not his dick, maybe this could've all been avoided. Josh and Mikaela would be just fine, and Jack would be his lonely, bitter self. No, he'd fucked up again, but this time it was much worse than just attacking Ariel. In the end, he hadn't really hurt her. He'd scared her, freaked himself out, but they'd both emerged from the incident unscathed. This time he'd caused serious damage, damage he'd never be able to forgive himself for.

Because no matter what Lillian had done, he still loved her—hated her with every breath he took, but loved her. Endlessly. And that was why he'd never be able to move past this. He should've killed her in the woods, destroyed her diseased mind and made her suffer for the damage she'd caused.

But he couldn't because he was weakened by his feelings for her. And yet, it wasn't as easy as letting someone else take her out because he knew he would never allow anyone else to hurt her either. If there was any saving grace for Jack, it was that Lillian hadn't acted alone.

When he and Josh had picked up the scent of Lillian and Mikaela, there'd also been the scent of her father, verification on what the rest of them had just learned right before Jack and Josh began their search.

Rodrick Lyons had people looking for Jack's mother ever since she'd disappeared, but when she'd died, he called off the search, finally trying to honor her wish of solitude. However, Rodrick had learned that a few of his investigators had taken it upon themselves to continue the search in hopes of collecting the large reward for her and her family's discovery. When he'd called Thomas to tell him this, he'd also informed him there was a paper trail of money transfers to Lillian's father.

The scheme had turned out to be much more elaborate than first assumed. Josh had been enraged, and Jack had used that as his opportunity to suggest Josh go after her father while he dealt with Lillian when they found them.

Jack wasn't worthy of his family's love or respect because he knew he'd save Lillian in the end, and that in and of itself was a betrayal to the men who loved and worked with him day in and day out.

"She's going to be fine, you know." Ariel's murmured words startled him, and he turned to face her.

"I hope so." Jack crossed his arms and rubbed them to comfort himself as he stared down at her.

He knew Ariel was referring to Mikaela, but Jack was worried about Lillian being stuck in the woods while the blaze was uncontained. Lillian's father's house had burned, and the area had smelled of an accelerant. Jack wasn't a fire investigator, but the incident reeked of arson. Fires weren't uncommon this time of year, but they'd gotten a lot of rain lately, and there hadn't been a storm last night to ignite the forest. If the house had succumbed to its demise from an unattended candle or an electrical issue, the area wouldn't stink of gasoline. And Lillian was still out there. Maybe the universe would smile on him and rid this world of her without his involvement. But even the thought of Lillian being hurt...

"How's Josh?" Ariel asked softly.

"He's a wreck." What else could he say?

"How are you?"

"Huh?" Jack rubbed his face with both hands to force his emotions to stay back. He wouldn't allow them free. Not right now.

Not ever. Anything he felt for Lillian would stay locked behind a vault, never to see the light of day. It was bad enough he loved her, but he'd be damned if he dwelled on that. He'd meant what he'd said in the woods. Lillian Caldwell was dead to him.

"Don't play dumb with me, Jack. I know you're hurting. You look like, well, you look like your wife just died and you're trying to pretend everything's okay."

"I don't have a wife." He crossed his arms.

"Your mate, then."

"I don't have a mate."

Ariel took a slow breath and watched him. She seemed as if she were looking for the right words to say, but Jack knew that was fruitless.

"You're hurting right now. You might never fully recover from what Lillian did to you. But please know that none of us... *none* of us blames you. You are as much of a victim here as Mikaela is."

When he tried to deny that, Ariel lifted her hand to stop his protest. "Her wounds are physical. Those are the kinds that heal the fastest. Yours are emotional and can be just as devastating."

"I don't care about me. It's Mikaela—"

"*I* care about you." Then she wrapped her arms around him in the tightest hug she'd ever given him.

Jack instinctually clutched her to him a little closer, finding the embrace more than comforting. It was a lifeline. "Everyone is important in this family, and that includes you, Jack."

"Thank you," he mumbled into her hair as he held her. He didn't fully believe her, but it was nice to hear.

"Hey, angel," Rob said beside Jack, so he let go of his brother's mate and stepped back.

"Hi, Robbie. Any news?"

"Yeah, one of the doctors just came out. All the tests they've run have been good, and it looks like they are both going to be fine." Rob smiled. "He said Mikaela is coming to now."

The relief was so profound that Jack would've buckled if his knees weren't locked.

"The investigative team that Lyons sent is headed here to talk to her. She's asked to speak to Josh."

Rob hesitated, rolling up on his toes

and back down before looking at Jack, saying, "And you."

"Me?" Why would she want to see him? Ah, hell. It was probably to warn him about Lillian. Mikaela didn't need to be concerned about him. She needed to focus on her recovery so she and the baby would be fine.

"Yeah, man. Josh is headed in there now. He said to give him a few minutes before you come in."

"Okay. I'm gonna grab some water, and then I'll go see her." He'd said it as an excuse to walk away from the concerned gazes of his brother and his brother's mate, and to buy the time Josh had asked for. Since they had Mikaela holed up in Josh's old room of the main house, he had to go downstairs to the kitchen to get his drink.

Unfortunately, it hadn't taken him long to walk down there, get some water, drink it, and walk back.

Or at least it had felt like only seconds to him. He knocked on the bedroom door and entered when he heard Josh call out the permission.

"Hey," he mumbled, looking at Josh and then Mikaela as he walked over to her.

He gently rubbed her upper arm before sitting in the chair beside the bed. Josh was seated on the other side of the bed, and several doctors walked around reading charts and looking very busy. The room was filled with machines—several of which Mikaela was hooked up to—that made it look as if this were an actual hospital room.

"Dad just stepped in while you were gone and said the fire next door is contained, so we won't need to worry about evacuating," Josh said as he nudged a little closer to his wife. He had both hands on her, and Jack couldn't blame him for needing that reassurance that she was alive.

Jack nodded. "That's good. It wouldn't have been fun trying to prep this place to minimize the damage before fleeing." He looked at Mikaela. She was covered with bruises and cuts, but the cuts didn't look as bad as he'd feared. She'd been covered in dried blood when they'd found her. "How are you feeling?" he asked her softly.

"Better now. They gave me some Demerol."

"Docs said it wouldn't hurt the baby. Now that she was conscious they wanted to keep her blood pressure down, so they gave her something for pain. They think when it wears off, she might be okay with just Tylenol."

"So you're a little loopy?" Jack asked, smiling at her. She gave him a goofy chuckle, and he pressed his lips together to keep from laughing at her.

"You could say that. I'm also sleepy, so Josh is going to make me take a nap."

"Kitten, you heard the doctor. You—"

"Yeah, yeah, yeah. I'm not complaining. I just need to clear something up." She looked at Jack, trying to flatten her expression, but just looking a little silly instead.

"Bro, she was just filling me in on what really happened, and you do need to hear this."

Jack stiffened in his seat, but didn't say anything. He wasn't sure if he could hear more hurtful things about Lillian. His heart just couldn't take it.

"Mr. Caldwell is who took me. Not Lillian." Mikaela waved her hand around, but then her focus stayed on her hand. "Heeey, where's my wedding wing?" She frowned and closed one eye as she looked at her hand. Then she opened that eye and closed the other. Did she think it'd reappear if she looked at it from a different angle?

"Doctors took it off, baby. I have it." Josh took that hand into his and rubbed it.

"Ooooh." She smiled at Josh and then looked at Jack. The seconds ticked by as she continued to stare at him, not saying anything. "What was I saying?"

It didn't matter what she was trying to tell him. He'd already known about Lillian's father's involvement. Jack just needed to placate her until the meds took her completely under. He steeled his heart before answering, "You were telling me about being kidnapped."

Her eyes popped open wide. "Right! Um, yeah, Lilly-man didn't take me. Her father is crazy, with a capital *craze*." She leaned toward Jack as if she was engrossed in an awesome story. "He beat me up and left some note. He dragged me back to his house and gave me something to knock me out. I never saw Lilly-man. I-I ka-member waking up, an' Lills was arguing with her father. She picked me up and mumbled something about helping me and getting us outta there." Mikaela shook her head slowly. "I don't think she had any idea what her father was doing to me. I think she was trying to help me."

Jack's heart was pounding so hard he just knew everyone in the room could hear it. Lillian might be innocent. His hands were shaking, and his mouth was suddenly dry. Oh God, he hoped she was.

Only because it'd lessen his guilt for what had happened to Mikaela. But the hole in his chest grew, his heart aching even more.

Even if Lillian hadn't kidnapped Mikaela, his judgment still couldn't be trusted. If he truly deserved her, he would've stood up for her, fought for her honor in the face of adversity, but he hadn't. He'd threatened to kill her. The guilt he'd felt when he believed he'd fallen for Lillian's lies didn't even compare to the devastating remorse he felt for not being there for and believing in his mate, or at least giving her the benefit of doubt. Just more proof that he was too damaged to be mated to anyone.

Mikaela's eyes rolled back, and she slumped against the pillow, out cold.

"We need to investigate this. It's possible Lillian's father set her up to make her take the fall," Josh whispered, unaware of his inner turmoil.

"I should've been the one to kill him," Jack growled.

"Too late. I'm gonna talk to Dad about this. Have him talk to the Lyons investigators to see what they can find before they leave."

Jack nodded. They needed the truth regardless of what it was, but he couldn't get lost in that right now. He needed to focus on what Josh was saying. "Any idea what'll happen with the Lyons family now that they know where we are?"

Josh sighed as he snuggled up against Mikaela. "Dad said he'd deal with it. I don't know what that means, but he and Jeffery were in some heated discussions just before I came in." He shrugged.

"Honestly, I don't give a shit about that right now. Mikaela and my baby are all that matter to me."

Jack stood up and pressed a chaste kiss against Mikaela's forehead. "I'm very happy she's okay, man. Get some rest." Jack hoped his expression was indifferent enough to be believable.

"We'll talk more about everything later."

Jack nodded, not really looking forward to some of the conversations his stubborn brother would be bringing up. He knew Josh wanted to discuss Lillian in depth, and Jack would because it would be expected of him. But Jack's mind was made up. He would pray that Lillian wouldn't be as cold as he'd first thought.

God, as he'd first believed.

But either way, he couldn't be with her. Either she was an evil creature he needed to avoid, or he was a heartless man who'd chewed up his mate and spit her out when he should've coddled and protected her. And what really hurt him now was, deep down, he knew the truth of what had happened today.

He was a heartless son of a bitch.

CHAPTER ELEVEN

LILLIAN HAD BEEN EXONERATED. In the weeks since Mikaela had been kidnapped and her father killed, she'd cooperated with the Woodses' investigators who'd worked the case. They'd verified what she'd told them, that she had no idea what her father had been up to and that he'd used her job with the Woods family to get better access to their property. Nowhere in the transactions and communications could they find a connection to Lillian and the rogue investigator who'd taken it upon himself to back her father in this insane scheme to expose the Woodses. She was relieved to be a free woman, but the investigation hadn't been her only obstacle.

She also had to bury her father, and

she'd had mixed emotions about that. There wasn't any love lost between them, and she hated him for what he'd done to Mikaela, but he was still her father. She'd buried him next to her mother's gravesite, and being near her mom also brought her emotions to the forefront. She was all alone and had no one to help her regroup. Her grandmother had come down for the funeral, but she hadn't stayed to console her. And if the investigation or the funeral hadn't brought her to the pits of hell, the fact that she was jobless and homeless had done the trick.

Since the fire had been rightfully ruled intentional, the insurance company wasn't going to cover the cost to rebuild. Her father had left her some money, so she'd be able to rebuild eventually, but she'd need to get a new business going again to create steady income once the money ran out. She'd already set aside the amount he'd made from harming the Woods family. No way was she going to profit from it, but she had no intention of giving it back to the creep who'd paid her father. That lowlife had been weeded out and was probably doing time on the reservation where the

Lyons family ruled. Lillian had contacted Mikaela about the money because she had an idea of how to spend it and wanted Mikaela's approval. If she hadn't agreed with the idea, then Lillian was going to insist on Mikaela deciding how to spend the money. She was the one most hurt out of this, and it was the least Lillian could do to make up for what her father had done to her neighbor.

And it was the need to discuss that money that forced Lillian to show up at the Woods estate this evening. Well, it was *Mikaela* who had insisted. She'd gone on and on about how she hadn't blamed Lillian for anything and that she wanted her to come back to work with them. She had even offered to let her stay at one of the cabins while her house was being rebuilt. The thought of not living in a hotel room in the next town was very appealing, but Lillian knew being on the estate again would be too much for her because she'd have to see *him*.

God, she missed Jack. He consumed her waking thoughts and her dreams. There wasn't a moment in the day that she hadn't ached for him. What started out as fun had turned into something so much more. And not just for her. He'd said that he loved her. He hadn't professed his love. He'd spat it out like it was an awful taste he couldn't get rid of, and that hurt. But she couldn't blame him.

He'd believed the worst about her. Mikaela had told her that Jack was now aware of the truth, yet he hadn't tried contacting her. Lillian had figured as much. She knew when she saw him last in the woods that he wouldn't ever let her near him again. He was both livid at her and at himself. He might accept the truth about her, but it was him he needed to forgive. And Lillian knew him well enough to know that wouldn't come easy.

She'd wait. Love didn't come with a user manual, but she knew if she truly loved him, she would never find another man who'd compare to her scaredy-cat. She just hoped in time he'd learn to accept how he was and how he felt about her. It was that hope that got her through the last couple of weeks and would continue to help her through the tough road she had ahead.

Lillian pulled up to the gate, which immediately opened, and drove the winding path to the main house. Just being so close to where Jack lived made her stomach do somersaults. After she parked and climbed the stairs, Jeffery greeted her at the door.

"It's lovely to see you again, Ms. Lillian. You look beautiful as always."

She smiled and let him take her jacket. "Mikaela is expecting me." She assumed he knew this already, but she felt as if she needed to explain why she was here. It was as if she was already an outsider, and that felt awful, too.

"Of course. She's in her office."

Lillian excused herself, not wanting to make small talk. She needed to get this visit over with and flee before she ran into Jack. She hoped like hell she'd at least get to see him from a distance, though, but she didn't want to cause him any unnecessary pain. She figured, in time, she might approach him, maybe do something as daring as she had when she'd first started her job here—hell, she'd been looking at that bra and thong set she'd worn her first day here, hoping he'd get to see it one day —but it was too soon for something like that.

She knocked on the door to Mikaela's office.

"Come in," she called out.

Lillian pushed the door open and slowly closed it shut. "Hi."

Thank God, Mikaela looked much better than she had the last time they'd seen each other. The lady before her now didn't have caked blood or bruises. A few lingering scrapes on her forehead and cheek were all that remained.

"Hey, girl." Mikaela walked up and hugged her. "Thanks for coming."

Lillian stepped out of the embrace and chuckled nervously. "You didn't give me much of a choice."

Mikaela winked at her just before she turned and headed to her desk. "I know." She picked up a flask of whiskey and poured a shot. "Now drink this."

"Why?" Lillian asked timidly as she stepped over to Mikaela. She took the shot glass and eyed it warily.

"Because you need to take the edge off."

That was no lie. She downed the shot without argument and sat down. Mikaela walked around and took her seat, too.

"So tell me your idea about the money," she said as she poured more liquor into that little glass.

Lillian waved her hand, trying to stop her. "That won't be necessary."

"That *will* be necessary. Two more."

What? "Are you trying to get me drunk?"

Mikaela chuckled. "I would never dream of such a thing. I'm just jealous I can't join you. This is girl talk, so we're making it fun."

Lillian felt a twinge of longing at the thought of just hanging out with friends and shooting the breeze over drinks. She'd never really had that before. She picked up the glass and downed the drink. She could just call a cab to come get her.

"Good girl. Now tell me your plans."

Lillian coughed as the burn of the whiskey went down, and then cleared her throat. "Well, I've been trying to come up with a way to spend the money so that you can at least get something out of the horrible thing that happened."

Mikaela sighed. "Listen, chick. I told you on the phone you have nothing to worry about. I do not blame you. *No one* blames you." The way Mikaela looked at her, she knew exactly whom the woman was stressing. Jack. She felt nerves tingling inside her at the thought of him. A reaction she'd better get used to.

Her enabler poured another shot and pushed the glass toward her. This time Lillian drank it without any more prodding.

"Can we just talk about the money?" She sounded as though she was begging, but she didn't care.

Mikaela nodded as she poured another drink. She didn't push it toward her, though, thank God. Lillian would be three sheets to the wind in ten minutes if Mikaela kept up this pattern.

"By all means."

Lillian fidgeted a little, but quickly covered her nervousness. She got the feeling Mikaela had that drink on the ready with the first sign of discomfort Lillian showed. "Since you're pregnant and needed medical attention, it became painfully clear there isn't a clinic close by. Um, so I was thinking we could start one out here. I-I know the money would in no way cover the costs of starting and running one, but I figured with yours and Krista's legal connections, and Ariel's chemical background and dealing with grants, you all could apply for federal funding. Since I have to rebuild the house and part of my plantation has been destroyed, I figured I could donate the land for the clinic to be housed. That way, no money would need to go toward purchasing additional land, nor would land have to be sacrificed that produces income for your family. I know this would be a major project, but with the dangers surrounding forestry work, I think it's a good idea to have something like this around here." And it would give her something to focus on. A job. A future. One that would keep her close to Jack, and help her to one day work her way back into his life.

Mikaela pushed the shot glass toward Lillian and smiled brightly. "I think that is a wonderful idea!"

Lillian exhaled the rest of the air she'd been holding in as she picked up the glass. She drank it greedily and placed the glass back on the table. "I'm so happy you like it. It'll be a huge job, but I think it would really be a wonderful feature for our community."

"Absolutely. I just have two favors to

ask, and I'll give you my backing, support, help, whatever is needed."

Uh-oh. Favors? That didn't sound good. What could she possibly want? Mikaela must have noticed the uneasiness that suddenly came over her because her bartender quickly poured another shot and pushed it toward her. Then it dawned on her.

"Do these *favors* have anything to do with you trying your best to get me wasted?"

Mikaela's smile was sly. She leaned forward on her elbows. "You could say that."

Shit. "So spill."

Mikaela steepled her fingers. "One, I want you to move here while your home is being rebuilt. It's insane for you to pay for a hotel indefinitely or get some crappy little rental. Two, while you're here, I want you to come to our dinners, starting tonight." She glanced at her watch. "Which starts in about ten minutes."

Panic raced through Lillian. Panic and elation. She would love to be closer to Jack all the time, but he wasn't ready for it. She knew he wasn't. It was going to take her time to ease him back into a relationship.

"You're thinking too hard. A simple yes

or no will do. Actually, only a yes will do. I mean, it *was* your father who took me against my will. I think it's the least you can do to make amends."

Lillian narrowed her eyes. "You already said that no one blames me for that."

"We don't. But I'm not above blackmail. Give me what I want, and I'll give you want you want. Besides, you know you want to be here, too. I'm just forcing your hand so you don't have to feel the guilt."

God, she was good. "Remind me never to go against you in court."

Mikaela chuckled. "Darlin', I'd eat you for dinner and still have room for dessert."

Lillian picked up the shot glass and said, "You can't eat me. I don't swing that way." Then she downed it.

Mikaela threw her head back and guffawed. "That's good. So do we have a deal?"

Lillian watched her for several seconds, trying to quickly weigh her options and knowing it wouldn't matter what she considered because her heart was pounding too hard for her brain to hear her thoughts.

"Yes."

Mikaela stood. "Oh, and a word of advice. If you want him, you're going to have to challenge him."

"What do you mean by that?"

Mikaela walked up to her and wrapped her arm around hers. "You're a woman. You can figure that out."

That was what she was afraid of.

———

"WHY THE FUCK are you trying to get me drunk?" Jack snapped, slightly slurring his words, as Josh pushed another glass of scotch in front of him. His brother had insisted on quitting work sooner than normal and getting an early start on drinks before dinner. Said some shit about needing to unwind. Right, as if Mikaela would let him take a load off like this right now. She was one bossy pregnant lady, and Jack knew Josh wouldn't do anything to push her buttons while she still had that bun in the oven.

"I'm not. I'm getting *me* drunk. Mikaela suggested it this afternoon, and by God, I'm not looking that gift horse in the mouth. I'm just bringing you along for the ride." Josh looked at him through the corner of his eye as he raised his glass to his mouth. "You could use a little break, too, man."

Jack grunted as he picked up his snifter and sipped. He'd refused to talk about Lillian after the results of the investigation had gone down. She'd been innocent all along, and he'd been a right bastard for not being there for her. If he was a man worthy of her, he'd—

"Hello? You're thinking again. I said to stop that shit. Everybody else will be here in a few minutes for dinner. It's not time to mope. You're doing enough of that shit when you're sober."

Jack chuckled. Josh was right. He'd been a bear to everyone since the kidnapping. He could just relax for the night. Tomorrow he'd be back to his cranky self. "You know, the last time I got drunk was when Lillian—" Jack stopped, his heart pounding at the thought of remembering the night he'd first made love to that woman. He missed her so much that at times he wondered how he'd be able to live life like this. Without her.

"Yeah, bro, I know. You should call her."

"Can't."

"You mean you won't. There's a difference, Jack."

Jack shook his head and downed the rest of his drink. If Josh expected him to discuss his feelings for Lillian, his brother would have to get him much drunker than he was now. He poured his own glass this time. The door opened, and his other brothers and father stepped in. He nodded at them as a greeting before tipping his glass to his lips.

"How's Mikaela?"

"Well that was a subtle subject change," Josh sighed, but then a crooked smile formed on his face.

"You can ask her yourself. I think I hear her coming now."

"Hi, son," Thomas said and clapped Jack on the shoulder before taking a seat at the table.

"Hey, Dad. I went online to place an ad —" Whatever else he was going to say died on his lips when the door opened. He saw Mikaela, but that wasn't who he scented. That smell was unmistakable and made his heart beat in double time. Then his Lilly stepped into view, and his heart just stopped.

"Fuck," he breathed.

Her gaze darted around the room, landing on everyone. She glanced at him a few times, but every time their eyes met, she looked away. God, she was beautiful.

And here.

"Well isn't this a pleasant surprise?" Thomas said as he stood up. "Come on in. Jeffery is about to bring out dinner. You two must be starving." He chuckled. "Well, one of you must be starving. The other might have to fight the other off for food."

"Ha-ha, Thomas," Mikaela said drily as she walked to the table. Lillian was right beside her. It looked as if she were ready to grab Mikaela if she left Lillian's side. Scared little thing. And his guilt came crashing down on him. She was timid because of him. Maybe if he wasn't tipsy, he could think of something clever to say. Damn Josh and his bad timing. He glanced at his drunk brother as Lillian moved to her seat and gritted his teeth. That fucker was grinning! Oh, holy hell. He looked at Mikaela, and she smirked at him. Those two were up to no good, and when Lillian stumbled with her chair, he realized she wasn't in any better condition than him.

"Are you fucking kidding me?" he barked at Josh. "Do you think getting us drunk is going to fix anything?"

Josh was sporting a silly grin. "Well, getting drunk worked that first night. Who knows what'll happen tonight?" He shrugged as he took another sip.

He was going to kill his brother. Kill him dead. In his sleep.

Mikaela grabbed the glass from her husband. "Your job here is done. Time for some coffee, mister."

Josh pouted, but then smiled at her. Damn, Jack wished he was as drunk as Josh appeared to be. This little setup would be easier to handle.

"How are you?" Krista asked Lillian.

"Um, okay. I mean, there's been a lot going on, but I'm okay." She glanced at Jack, and he couldn't stop staring at her. Her cheeks turned a luscious shade of pink under his perusal.

Jeffery walked in with one plate of food and placed it in front of Mikaela. In his other hand, he held a bottle of whiskey. He placed it on the table and chuckled as he retreated.

"What the hell's going on?" Jack asked.

"Oh, Josh thought it'd be fun if we all played a drinking game before eating. We'll each say something truthful, and if you don't agree with the statement, you have to take a drink. Except Mikaela. My grandbaby needs to go ahead and eat." Jeffery returned with another bottle of whiskey and several shot glasses. He passed them out and started pouring everybody's drinks. Josh was laughing out loud and clapping his hands. Fuck.

"I told you that shit in private," Jack spat.

"Well, little brother, you should've manned up before now." Josh winked at him. Yep, he was going to fucking kill him dead, dead, dead. And Jack wasn't going to wait until he was asleep to do it.

"I'll start." Thomas rose his glass and looked around the room. "I am completely and totally happy with where my personal life is right now." He sat the glass down and looked at Jack.

Shit.

Jack looked at Lillian. She picked up her glass and sipped. No one else drank from theirs. He glared at his father and slammed his drink back, feeling the burn.

Jeffery refilled Jack's glass while Mikaela refilled Lillian's.

"Mine turn!" Josh bellowed. "I tolds my mate that I wuv her today." He leaned over and kissed Mikaela sweetly.

Double shit. Jack couldn't even look at Lillian. He just drank his punishment and put the glass on the table. Jeffery was quick on the refill. Jack wasn't sure how much of this he could take.

"I have one," Toby announced. "I can't wait to start a family and have kids of my own."

He was related to a bunch of evil, sadistic bastards.

"Hear, hear!" Thomas said. "I'd love to have a house full of grandkids."

Jack groaned as he drank the next shot, but couldn't help looking up this time. Lillian was watching him as she sipped hers. Her eyes looked a little red. Were those tears? Damn it. If this was upsetting her, his family had really crossed the line. He could take the abuse, but he wouldn't sit here and let her suffer.

"Cat got your tongue, huh?" Lillian huffed at him.

"What?"

"Nothing, Tigger." So those weren't tears. She wasn't sad. Now that he was really studying her, she looked pissed.

Rob laughed. "Well, look, she still has some spirit left in her. My turn, people." He raised his glass and looked right at Lillian. "I have never insulted anyone with cat names."

"Hey!" Ariel said. "That's not fair. I think I've done that before."

Krista shrugged. "I probably have, too. No biggie, sis, one drink won't hurt us."

The three women in the room who were not pregnant swallowed their shots.

"I think it's my turn," Lillian said. She lifted her glass, and it sloshed to the side a little. She was definitely past the tipsy stage and barreling full steam ahead to drunkenness. "My mate refuses to talk to me."

Jack slammed his glass down. "I'm not refusing to talk to you, Lillian. I—"

"Well, thuffering thuccotash, Sylvester, you have one hell of a way of showing it."

The room erupted in laughter. Jack pushed his fists onto the table and stood. He glared at her across the table. "You are insufferable. I haven't seen you beating down my door either."

Lillian stood on wobbly legs. "What'd you expect? Me to call you and say, 'Hello Kitty,' or, or, or, '*Heavens to Murgatroyd, Snagglepuss*, but are you ever going to acknowledge me again?'"

Jack stormed around the table and grabbed her by her arms. "Acknowledge you? There's not a day that goes by that I don't think of you."

"Well you have one funny way of showing it, Snowball!"

"That's it!" Jack roared. He picked her up and threw her over his shoulder. She beat against his back as he turned to face his family. They were all grinning like the Cheshire Cat. *Fuck!* Now he was doing it, too. "I hope you all are happy. We'll be in my cabin setting some things straight."

"We'll see you *both* at breakfast," Thomas called out as Jack stormed out of the room.

Mikaela squeaked out, "Don't forget what I said!" just as the door shut. Whatever the hell that meant.

Yep, his family was evil.

CHAPTER TWELVE

LILLIAN FELT herself being tossed onto the bed in Jack's cabin. If she weren't so drunk, she'd make a run back to the main house and kiss Mikaela on the mouth. Her and her favors. Lillian hadn't planned on pushing Jack to his limit, not yet, but once she got a little liquid courage in her and was presented the opportunity, she couldn't help it. Her true nature had pushed through. And thanks to Mikaela, she knew if she pushed Jack to the edge, all he'd be able to do was fall over.

And boy, had he fallen. He looked downright viral as he reveled in it.

"You think you can push me around and take what you want?" Oh yeah, he could, but she wasn't stupid enough to let him know that. "You owe me an apology."

Jack whipped his shirt over his head and reached for the placket of his jeans. "I'm sorry." He looked down as he pushed his pants off.

"That's it? You're sorry?" She was going to make sure she pushed all his buttons before this night was through.

"No, that's not it. You're not naked. You better get that way now if you want to keep those clothes for another day."

She bounded up to her knees and put her fists at his hips. "You have some nerve, big guy. If this is wooing me, you need to work on your social skills."

He stalked over to her, grabbed her shirt, and ripped if off her. She gasped.

"I hate you, Jackson Woods!"

"I hate you, too, Lillian Caldwell!"

He crushed his mouth to hers and kissed her with so much force she had to struggle to get her tongue into his mouth. They each fought for control of the kiss while Jack reached down and yanked her pants with enough force that they tore as she was thrust against him. She broke away from the kiss and glared at him.

"Quit ruining my clothes."

"I warned you." He reached for her pants again, but she pushed him away and rolled off the bed to the other side.

"Look here, Jackson, we're doing this on my terms." She held her hand out in a defensive maneuver.

"You can think whatever you want, Lillian. But you know how this is going to end. I'll be fucking you, and you'll be submitting to me. You've pushed me too fucking far."

Oh God, did her pussy just throb? His words shouldn't have been such a turn-on. But she was more turned on now than she ever remembered being with him. She licked her kiss-swollen lips and slowly pushed her pants down and shrugged off the remnants of her torn shirt and bra. She left her panties on just to tease him a little more.

"Fuck, Lilly, I love your breasts." He started climbing on the bed toward her, but she backed away.

"If you want me, Jack, you'll have to do what I say."

He stopped and growled at her. "Stop fucking pushing me! You don't understand how bad my lion wants to dominate you."

Oh, she figured as much. Hell, she was banking on it, but she wanted him completely lost. Only when he let go of all his control would he be able to accept himself. She was doing this for him. For her. For the both of them. She was aware that this might backfire on her, but she was making it up as she went along, and somewhere inside her, she knew she needed to test him.

"Oh please, Tom, you couldn't dominate Jerry."

He roared and dove for her. She jumped, but wasn't fast enough. He pinned her against the wall.

She tried pushing him off her, but then his mouth landed on the sensitive spot where her neck met her shoulder.

And then he bit. Hard.

"You will fucking submit, Lilly."

"Screw you, big guy. You want it? You'll have to take it. I ain't giving you shit."

"I'll be taking you all night, showing you who you belong to," he taunted.

Please, please, please, she chanted to herself, but she said, "Big words for such a scaredy-cat."

He lifted her easily and whirled them. He pushed the top half of her onto the bed and let her legs dangle off the edge. He held her down with one hand between her shoulder blades and grabbed the scrap of lace that was cocooned between her ass cheeks.

"You may leave these on. For now," Jack rasped.

And oh Lord, if he wasn't tracing the line of her panties, making her pussy and her pucker both contract.

"I may do whatever I damn well please, Azrael. You'll need the help of Gargamel's wizardry if you think you're going win this."

He leaned over her, his lips brushing over her ear. "The Smurfs, really?"

"I told you, I had a ton of them."

She used his momentary distraction as the opportunity to strike. She bucked beneath him and twisted at the same time, catching his arm at the crook of his elbow, and managed to break free.

Until he pinned her down again, only this time she was facing him. He grabbed her shoulders and pushed her farther up the bed. Now she was fully lying on the mattress, no part of her hanging off it.

"You're trying my patience, Lilly," he growled. His head descended, and whatever protest she was about to make died when he sucked her nipple into his mouth.

Her back arched, and she moaned. The feel of Jack's hot mouth encasing her was too distracting for her to fight back. Besides, she hadn't been fighting him to stop him from fucking her. She was challenging him as Mikaela had suggested—or with what she hoped was the right interpretation of what she'd suggested.

Jack groaned, and the vibrations against her breast traveled straight to her clit. And she couldn't wait for him to put his mouth there.

Ugh, but she needed to make sure she kept his need amped up as high as she could get it, not focus on him satisfying her aching body. When he let go of her breast and nibbled his way down her body, she fisted her hands in his hair, stopping his progress.

"Let go, Lilly. I want to taste what belongs to me."

"Then roll over."

"No," he snapped. He tried lowering his head again, but she held on to his hair. His head popped back. "Lillian, you will do as I say."

"Jackson, you will have to prove to me that you are worthy of my submission."

He hissed at her, his fangs descending, eyes narrowing. There. That's what she wanted. She wanted him feral.

"Come on, baby," she cooed. "You know you want me."

He threw his head back and roared, the sound making her shiver. Lillian shifted into her feline form and used her claws to yank herself out from under him. Once she was free, she shifted back, her torn panties falling off her.

He growled at her as he glared into her eyes. "You're cheating, mate."

"You have to earn the right to call me that, Jackson."

He pounced, and she grabbed his shoulders. They grappled, and Lillian found herself wedged between his side and the mattress. She bit him, and he roared. She pushed lower and nipped his hip.

He bolted up and grabbed her thigh.

But it was too late. Her target was now in her sights.

She dragged herself the last bit to his cock and sucked him deeply into her mouth. Jack's growling turned into a deep-rooted groan, his grip on her leg lessening briefly. He thrust up into her mouth.

"Yes, baby, like that. God, Lilly, that's so good."

She sucked him harder, but her rhythm faltered when the hands on her legs suddenly tightened, and she moved. She kept sucking his cock, though, so Jack wouldn't succeed at pulling her off him.

And then she realized his true agenda in making her move. She felt hot breath bathe her exposed thigh and moaned around his cock. He'd managed to pull her completely on top of him, her pussy was now in front of his face. She instinctively rotated her hips, not sure if she was trying to entice him to taste her or because she was so turned on she couldn't help but move. It didn't matter. When she felt the first lick of his tongue, her fingernails dug into his thighs and she sucked harder.

He gave as good as he got. Jack licked and sucked every inch of her pussy, the sounds of him eating her out driving her just as mad as the feel of him owning her. She sucked her finger into her mouth alongside his shaft and then traced it down, lining the seam of his sac, swirling along his perineum, and then probing at his pucker. At first he stilled and stiffened, but she sucked him harder as she gently pressed. When he relaxed, the tip of her finger breached his barrier, and she sucked him harder and slid it in.

"Fuck, Lilly," Jack breathed on her clit before losing that last bit of control he held on to.

He shoved two fingers into her, fucking her with those two as she fucked him with her one. She knew she'd found his prostate when he bucked and moaned. She eased back, not wanting to push him over the edge just yet. She sucked him hard, and he fucked her harder. Then he drew on her clit, and she screamed around his dick as her pussy clenched his fingers.

When the stars faded, she pulled her finger out of his ass and let go of his cock. She turned to face him. He was panting, his cock swollen, wet, filled with blood. And she couldn't wait for him to take her.

"You think you deserve me now?"

He didn't answer. Not verbally any-way. He growled as he pushed himself up and grabbed her. He flipped her over onto her hands and knees and shoved her shoulders flat onto the bed, leaving her ass high up in the air. His body encased her. His mouth found her ear.

"I know I do. You belong to me, and I want to hear you say it."

"Why don't you make me scream it?" she taunted.

He growled at her. "You will be screaming more than just that, Lilly."

He pushed into her with no warning, and she did scream. He felt so hard, hot, good. *Right.* He bit her shoulder as he pounded into her, fucking her harder than he'd ever taken her before, and all she could do was accept it, accept him. Her orgasm built lightning fast, and she was screaming again with the force of it.

"Say it!" Jack ordered.

And then she finally gave him what he wanted. "I'm yours, Jack. Always. God, I love you so much."

"Lilly," he yelled as he reached that state of nirvana and joined her in bliss.

She was shaking and panting, but as the clouds lifted from her orgasmic haze, she was finally able to make out the mumbling, the chanting from Jack.

"I love you, Lilly," he repeated over and over.

He kissed her shoulder and eased out of her, but he didn't move away. He pulled her into his arms and held her, kissed her hair, stroked her arm, and rocked her against him.

"I'm so sorry I doubted you." Jack's voice cracked. "I don't deserve you, Lilly, but I don't think I can stay away anymore. I love you so much. Will you please forgive me? I'll beg, do whatever you want. Please, just say you'll have me. Don't leave."

Lillian lifted up onto one elbow and looked down at him. "I love you, Jackson Woods. Warts and all. I know you can be very opinionated and hard to live with at times, but I wouldn't have it any other way. You push, but I push back. Do you think you can live with that?"

Jack smiled at her and traced his finger along the column of her throat. "I know I can. As long as you stop with the cat jokes." He cringed theatrically.

Lillian smirked. "I'll try." Then she frowned as she felt her neck. "Did you bite me again?"

He looked chagrined. "Yes, I'm sorry. I got carried away."

"Hmm... I'm not feeling very well."

"What? Oh shit, what's wrong?" Jack leaned up and held her to him while his eyes darted back and forth between hers.

"I think I've got cat scratch fever."

She couldn't help it. She laughed before she got it all the way out, and laughing felt pretty dang good.

She could get used to it.

"Oh, you will, Lilly. You will."

EPILOGUE

Thomas Woods sat against the oak tree where his mate was buried. He always came out here when he needed to talk to her or to think about their family. He missed her like crazy. Some days were easier than others, but lately he'd been aching to have her near him, so he'd been making the trip out here more often. He always stopped by Eric's grave first to visit his youngest son, but it was his visits with his mate that always drained him.

"Hello, beautiful," he breathed as he caressed the exquisite headstone. "I talked to your brother again today. He still feels awful for what happened to Mikaela and pledged to ensure our safety would be his top priority.

"He sends his love, by the way." Thomas chuckled as he sat down beside his wife's grave. "Prick, was always a thorn in my side, but you know that. At least he's promised to protect our sons' decision to stay here. Oh, sweetheart, you'd be so proud of them. None of them wishes to return to the plantation in Colorado. They all feel their rightful place is here, the home you created for them.

"You'd be pleased to learn that the women our sons have chosen as mates have taken on a new project. They are trying to build a clinic on part of Caldwell's land that borders the main road. It'll be a huge undertaking, but I think it's a wonderful plan. It was Lillian's idea."

Thomas looked up at the midmorning sky and breathed deeply. "She's good for our Jackson. I was worried about him. He seemed so hard. Still does. But she doesn't put up with his attitude." He half smiled, thinking about her feisty little attitude, too. "Yes, she'll definitely stay toe-to-toe with him.

"One of the great things about doing this clinic is it'll give Ariel a proper lab for her to conduct her research. Granted, she'll still have to travel to the university to facilitate her projects, but she will be able to do some work here as well. I know when she's gone for extended periods of time, Robert goes stir-crazy. And her sister, Krista, worries, too."

He leaned into the headstone. "Krista is such a character. She seems so shy one minute and then fierce the next. Definitely has a mother-hen quality to her. Toby has been talking to me about proposing to her. I think our boys are so focused on the mating aspect that they don't really think about the women's need for a ring." Thomas smirked. "I remember making that mistake. Remember that, sweetheart? You left wedding magazines lying round the house. Guess I need to share that story with our boys, too.

"But Joshua put a ring on Mikaela's finger at his first opportunity. They are so happy, darling. Well, Joshua has learned very quickly that a pregnant woman is not one to argue with. He's done very well and is tending to all her needs. He's only happy when she's happy, which is how it should be."

Thomas felt his face light up. "I can't wait until they have that little baby. Can you believe it? We're going to be grandparents! I still have to pinch myself when I think about that. They were the first to decide not to return to Colorado, but said they'd revisit the topic if they were having a girl because of the rarity of a female birth in the Lyons bloodline. They drove into town yesterday for Mikaela's monthly checkup and did an ultrasound to check on the baby's growth. That little angel is doing just fine. The doctor asked them if they wanted to know the sex. And they said no! Can you believe that? Guess we'll just have to wait and see if they have a girl or not."

Thomas looked at his watch. "Well, beautiful, I should probably get back to the house. Jeffery is preparing our lunch. I have breakfast with the boys—because the girls think eating breakfast that early is asinine—and dinner with everybody, but lunchtime is mine and Jeffery's time to visit. He's the brother I never had, though he'd never let his sense of duty get in the way of that." Thomas chuckled. "But I make him at lunch. He's getting much better at unwinding with me. I'm sure having a baby in the house will frazzle him enough to make him lose some more of his properness."

Thomas heard a rustling in the bushes and turned to see Jeffery stepping out. "Thought I'd find you here, Tom."

"Hey, Jeff, just talking about you to Lina."

Jeffery smiled at Thomas while he stood. "Lunch is ready."

Thomas nodded at him and turned to the gravestone. "Goodbye, sweetheart. I think we did pretty well with our boys," he whispered.

Jeffery chuckled. "You say that now, but wait until you talk to Joshua. He's been on the phone all morning with Mikaela's doctor trying to bribe her into telling him the sex of their baby. Mikaela is going to be furious when she finds out."

Thomas groaned. "I hope he has a boy who will be just as ornery."

Jeffery slapped Thomas on the back as they headed away from the gravesite. "From your mouth to God's ears, my friend. From your mouth to God's ears.

LIKE YOUR HOT alpha men with a side of danger? The Bang Shift Series contains full-length, contemporary romantic suspense novels, featuring mercenaries, mechanics, and the mafia! Start this hot, wild ride with **Brody**, the first book in the Bang Shift Series. FREE on all retailers!

———

WANT TO DIVE INTO A HOT, romantic comedy series? Tender Tarts features strong heroines in all kinds of situations, from crushes on their bosses to billionaires to sports starts! Start this totally sexy and often funny series with **Super Hot Supervisor**. It's FREE on all retailers!

———

HEY, y'all!

Thank you for reading my book. :) If you enjoyed it, I'd be very grateful for a review. If you didn't like it, then share that, too... as long as your review is honest, that's all that matters.

And ice cream. Ice cream matters, too.

Want the latest scoop? Be sure to sign up for my Newsletter! I mean, it's not as yummy as ice cream, but nothing ever is.

Xoxo,

Mandy

Surrounded by Temptation

Surrounded by Secrets

Young Adult written as M.W. Muse

Goddess Legacy

Goddess Secret

Goddess Sacrifice

Goddess Revenge

Goddess Bared

Goddess Bound

 Mandy Harbin is a *USA Today* Bestselling author who loves creating stories that explore the complexities of everyday relationships...with some kissing thrown in. She is a Superstar Award recipient, Reader's Crown and Passionate Plume finalist, and has achieved Night Owl Reviews Top Pick distinction many times. She also writes young adult romance as M.W. Muse because teens like kissing, too.

After graduating college and working many years in technology, she threw caution to the wind and began studying writing at the UALR. Years of trashed manuscripts and rejections eventually led to contracts and representation. With over thirty books published, she now serves on the board of her local writing chapter.

Mandy lives in a small, Arkansas town with her husband and their bossy dog, enjoying her own happily ever after...with some kissing thrown in.

www.mandyharbin.com

9 781941 467527